rosa

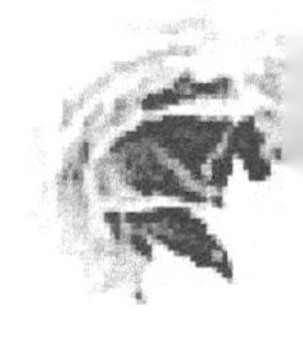

the driftless unsolicited novella series

Technologies of the Self	Haris A. Durrani
Faith Healer	Victoria G. Smith
Girling	C. Kubasta
Rosa	Barbara de la Cuesta

The Driftless Unsolicited Novella Series

rosa

BARBARA DE LA CUESTA

Brain Mill Press
Green Bay, Wisconsin

Published in the United States by Brain Mill Press.
Print ISBN 978-1-942083-83-2
EPUB ISBN 978-1-942083-86-3
MOBI ISBN 978-1-942083-84-9
PDF ISBN 978-1-942083-85-6

Cover art: No. 822 from the series "Phonography" by Matt Gold. © Matt Gold.
Cover design by Ampersand Book Design.

www.brainmillpress.com

Published by Brain Mill Press, the Driftless Unsolicited Novella Series publishes those novellas selected as winners of the Driftless Unsolicited Novella Contest each year.

to all my English students

Contents

rosa

PART ONE

Rosa puts the ric [illegible]
her feet up. Her b [illegible]
start of another [illegible] ...eeks after the
last. The front do[illegible] rings. She hopes it isn't Mondo's social worker—Mondo is in jail again until the start of April—or anyone like that, who usually come to the front. *Que entren*, she calls through the screen. It isn't a social worker; it's little Esmeralda, from the Mexican store. She comes in shyly when invited and sits primly across from Rosa on the divan with a notebook in her lap. Three years ago she was in Rosa's catechism class and was notably smarter and better mannered than any child she had ever taught the Salve Maria and the Padre Nuestro.

It's about a project for her fifth grade, says the little girl. She needs to interview an older person. Ah, Rosa feels old. Do I need to get up?

No, you sit right there and I ask you questions. Hah, like the social worker, she tells herself. No, this child used to sort through red beans on the floor of her papa's bodega. Hokay, she says. What kind of questions?

Well, about your life: where you were born, about your childhood, how you came here.

Rosa's childhood. Well that might be looked at, unlike some other parts.

So the little girl picks up her pencil, and Rosa sighs and begins the tale, up to the hard parts. Those unreel before her nights…

It was my aunt raised us. My mother died. There were four of us, she begins. My aunt, she cook for us in great pots on a petroleum stove behind the house, or in the big wood oven in the shed. You never knew what was in that pot… shreds of meat when we had some, and roots, and *verdes*. Each of us big ones have to feed a little one before we eat.

And then she boil the wash in another pot and hang it over the chicken coop. There was nothing like a washing machine in those days. Or even electric.

Did you ever have any fun?

Well, we children hunt eggs, and every Sunday we each have an egg fried in grease and put on stiff white dresses to walk in a line behind my aunt and uncle to Mass… You have to walk very carefully, because if you scuff your shoes you can't go out to play after.

My aunt is very strict, but we together, we sisters. We sleep in one big bed, and my brother, who was little then, sleep in my aunt's bed. She make him her baby. She don't have any children her own.

Was it a farm, where you lived?

A very small farm. All the family live on the same street. We have some chickens, and a pig they kill at Christmas. My other uncle have a cow; so we have all the milk we want, and curd for butter and white cheese.

A mile away there is an *abasto*, like your papa have. We girls was sent there with our pockets full of coins when the flour run out, or to buy canned meat. The big market is twenty kilometers away. There, we go in the horse cart with my uncle once a month. We have salt cod part of the month, and sometimes a chicken; when that run out we eat beans and rice. We live there till I am eleven and our father want us back. Were you happy? the little girl asks.

Was she happy? She must have been, because when her father came and took them all to run a household in that big brick half-built house in Ciudad Jardin, while he worked building houses—bringing home the scrap bricks to finish their own house—that was when the sadness began, the fear she doesn't see her way to telling this little questioner about. No, she can't, she just can't...So she heaves herself up, saying something about coffee, and goes to the kitchen to boil some water and set out some Goya biscuits, and of course Laureano comes in from whatever he's doing and wants coffee too. We'll talk more another time, says the girl, like a little woman already.

Yes, they will talk more, she promises; and from that afternoon on the thoughts of those years start to file past her mind's eye—as she was going to bed that night and even next morning dressing for work. She wonders for the first time why her father ever wanted them back? Three girls and a baby. It wasn't as if they could help him in his building projects. Like Laureano, he had his half-repaired cars, old washing machines, kitchen sinks, unfinished rabbit coops all around the house waiting for his attention. Their aunt had taught them all to cook, but they even forgot how to do that around him. Ah, well, she'll think of something nicer to tell the little girl next time she comes.

II.
Wolfie

On the bus the next day going to the sisters on Newtonville Road, she picks out Wolfie's window in the Glengarden Arms. Someone must have told. They never send her to Wolfie now. It's been months. The dreadful Irishwoman goes now, and Rosa is certain she is rough and cruel. It must be her who told, but how can she have known? Certainly Wolfie wouldn't have told her even if he could talk. Probably the Irish had their *santeria* like the Puerto Ricans. You could see it in their divining eyes.

With Wolfie she always sat on the edge of the tub and he put his hand up her skirt and into her panties, caressing her shyly, apologetically. So sorry, he seemed to say. Was he apologizing to her for touching, or for not being able to properly carry out this seduction, which, though he didn't know it, was as thrilling to her as any caress since Mondo's father's in that first year before he turned mean? Certainly more thrilling than Laureano's pumping. But she had been a girl then, when Mondo's father...

His name was Alejandro. Even his name had thrilled her once. Such an idiot. She certainly can't tell the little girl about Alejandro. But the babies... It would be a pleasure to tell her about the babies. She remembers waiting for Mondo's birth, how she pampered herself, oiling her skin and sitting in the sun outside the little house Alejandro was building for them in the forest in Xoyatla. Of all the building men in her life Alejandro was the finest. An artist. He built a boat once that won a prize from that museum committee. He carved it out of mahogany; it was ten feet long and sat on display in the patio of the museum in the capital—still does as far as she knows. She used to lie in the hammock watching him build, admiring the trueness of his corners as he set the windows in. A black man, he could work in the sun all day. Mondo would be a beautiful honey-colored baby, she knew as she waited.

Yes, the beautiful Alejandro turned mean. How can a body be as ugly as Clifford's and as thrilling as Alejandro's? Or any of his brothers and sisters', even his mother and father's. It's what held her there in Loiza where he was from. They were so happy and so free. They carved coconut shells and they lazed about in hammocks and sang and played guitars. And there was plenty of fruit in the trees and fish in the sea. Every morning, not very early, they "walked" the dugout boats down the beach, advancing the prow and the stern alternately, over the sand and into the softly curling waves; then stuck up a little sail and lay in the bottom with a line hung over and tied about their ankles to alert them of a fish to pull in. And it was so warm you never had to wrap yourself up in wool blankets like in Xoyatla.

Xoyatla was the chilly forest and misty mountain. The mist didn't rise off the mountain until eleven in the morning. There the tribes lived. Rosa, though she would never mention it to anyone, was a tribal person. Her people were squat and silent and hardworking. They never lay about and sang. The only place they ever sang was in church on holidays.

Was it living among them in the forest that turned him mean? Or the drink? By the time Mondo was born he had finished the house, and for a year they lived among her people. The baby, Mondo, was wrapped like a little package in wool blankets she wove herself. Mornings when she unwrapped him he was fiery red, covered with rashes. To heal him, they went often to Loiza, where he could sleep in a hammock with nothing on.

His pee went right through the loose weave. She often thought the Blakey sisters, that she used to care for sometimes on a night shift, and whose wet bedclothes she changed three times a night, might better sleep in hammocks. The people of Loiza not only slept in hammocks, they even had their babies in them. There she drew the line. Mondo was born in a bed with her aunt in attendance. Eva was born a year later in the clinic where Rosa was being treated for the broken jaw Alejandro gave her and the fall on the floor that brought on the birth three weeks early.

III.

The Sisters

She gets off at the sisters' corner. Actually, of the three, only Winnie lives there anymore; Megan and Adie have been moved to a nursing home, and Winnie's there alone with her brother Leo, who mostly cares for her. All but her bath; she also spends the afternoons at the Sunshine Club.

When she lets herself in, Winnie and her brother are shouting in the bathroom: she has a great gaping wound where it rubs her and she won't take it off, yells Leo. What? What? Rosa cries. Her girdle. She won't take it off. She sleeps in it.

Winnie hated anyone "messing in me panties," or in her girdle now lately. She was cold, she kept saying.

Yesterday she put her shoes and stockings in the oven to warm them up, nearly burned the house down, he tells Rosa. It's eighty degrees in here for heaven's sake!

I just work around it. We see, Rosa soothes. She starts the bath and turns on the bathroom heater. Nice and warm, she tells Winnie, and leaves the girdle and nightgown on while she induces Winnie to step in the tub.

Winnie sits in the bath chair, and Rosa cups the warm water in her hand and pours it over Winnie's swollen, purple legs. It's the circulation makes her cold. She peeks under the ruched-up nightgown into the borders of the girdle, sees no gaping wound, only some chafed skin where it's rubbed her. Winnie allows her to unhook the lower part and wash under, drying carefully before she hooks it up again. Then the upper part, gently removing the nightgown meanwhile. I'll wrap your shoulders in this warm towel now, she tells Winnie. They know what they need, these old ones. Leo should have more patience.

Still, how could she fault him? He'd promised all three sisters he'd never send them to nursing homes. And kept it for years, paying for home aides and finally moving back into the house to mostly care for Winnie, taking her to the bathroom every few hours and cooking her meals; the other two he visits regularly, though none of the three know who he is for sure.

Did you come with the bread and eggs? she asks Leo after Rosa has powdered and dressed her for a January day in the middle of a warmish October…

We always take a cracked wheat and a rye, and brown eggs, a half dozen, Winnie says.

Yes, ma'am, Leo says. They're in the kitchen. Rosa seats Winnie in a wing chair at the bridge table, where she'll play a couple games of gin rummy with Leo. Her memory of the game is accurate and canny. While they play, she always calls Leo "Clarence," her long-dead husband's name. He'll fix her lunch then and take her to the Sunshine Club for the afternoon.

IV.
Blood

She is right about the dragging in her womb. The clots start rushing out of her as soon as she leaves Winnie, and by the time she gets to Clifford Onderdonk, she has soaked the two pads she put on as a precaution. At least it isn't always twice a month anymore, or always so heavy as that last day she saw Wolfie—a day the cramping always brings back to her:

Wolfie sitting in his bath chair and she leaning over him, his hand, his clever hand up her skirt and into her panties, discovering her soaked pad and pushing it aside and her womb leaping, bringing her, bringing her, just needing to find her nipple with his mouth for it to happen, and the clots rushing out of her, staining his hand and the bathwater and the towel she was sitting on. She remembers how respectful and apologetic he always was. Asking her forbearance as if only he was stealing a pleasure, how unembarrassed he was about her period. Oh, she can remember. She can remember that whole day. It was the day that spaceship was going round and round in the sky, the day of Adie's hundredth birthday and the mayor's coming to the Sunshine Club; and she'd had to do two shifts practically in a row; and Priscilla was hit by a car riding home from the sisters.

Agotado, how she'd felt at the end of that day, carrying about her dragging womb, feeling Wolfie's hands on her long after they were gone, the way she used to feel Alejandro's *pene* even when it wasn't there, touching her womb, deep, deep, bringing on the cramp, the flow.

When we leave my aunt's to go to my father, my poor aunt was so unhappy, she tells little Esmeralda the next time she comes.

Because she never had any of her own. My uncle had to start taking her to doctors. She went to bed and wouldn't get up from the day we left. Rosa has identified this as the reason for The Sadness that had descended on her family.

She was sad because you went? Yes, my uncle say she was never the same again. But we did go back. Two of us, later. My little brother, Tito, was the first. He run away from my father late one night and go straight to my aunt's and crawl into the big bed with her and my uncle. And I went back, much later. With my two children.

And you were happy then, at your aunt's? What an astute child. Rosa has thought it over and decided they were good years, both when she was a girl and later with the children. They grumbled and did what Aunt Tina wanted. It felt very safe and good, yes.

But I keep *thinking* I not happy when I go back. Because I think I love my husband still. I use to hang on to my children and cry and cry. My aunt hate that. Clean them up if you love them so much. So I would work and forget.

Your husband was bad to you, so you left. Yes... She must not tell the child about these things.

Two years ago my father got drunk and hit my mother and we moved out, the girl tells her then. We went to live with my uncle in West New York.

Rosa is shocked. She never heard about this. Ah, this child knows things, she thinks. But you come back?

Yes, but he knows she'll leave him again if he hits her. All kinds of bad things happened while we were gone. His cousins came and moved in with him and stole his truck and a bunch of money. My mother had to straighten out everything.

Dear child. She knows more than I ever did at that age. My poor Aunt Tina is stiff from the arthritis and hardly can see with the cataracts when I go back, she tells the little girl. She work as hard as before though.

They sit at the kitchen table for these sessions now, and the little girl writes these bits of Rosa's life in a blue school notebook. Eventually Laureano comes in and wants coffee, so Rosa boils the milk and tints it with the breakfast coffee saved in a thermos Eva gave her for Christmas. Laureano likes to tell the little girl things, too, about the houses he's built. As if he is jealous of all the attention being paid to her, Rosa. How silly he is.

Yes, it is Tito, the baby, oddly, the one who ran back to their aunt, that gets the idea of Lowell, Massachusetts, in his head, Rosa tells the little girl.

Some friends of his working there. He talk about it for months... I remember little Mondo try to say the word... Mass-a-chu-setts. And then one day he just go. Tito. He work in a shoe factory, and mop hospital floors at night.

And so little by little I get the courage to come too. With Mondo and the new baby still in diapers. I work in the shoe factory till it close, then I pack apples in cartons, out past Billerica. And I live with my two babies in one of Tito's rooms at the back of a tenement by the river. It is so sad in the city. There are no flowers, only big brick buildings with windows you can't see into they are so dirty, and streets and sidewalks. Then I find the place in Billerica. It is over a store, and I see the green grass and gardens and *huertas* . . .

Orchards, says Esmeralda. Yes, orchards. And Mondo go to a little school on a yellow bus that stop every day in front of the house. And he and Eva run around and play with the children from the store. And I buy that *mueble* over there—Rosa points to the oak cupboard where she keeps her best dishes and the cans of *galletas* Goya that Mondo painted flowers on for her, and the coffee mill brought from home.

And I walk. There is no yellow bus for me. I walk seven miles to the work and seven miles home.

And each month I can buy something better: a Slumber King bed for me and new mattress for the children, and a big lamp that Mondo and Eva break, so I have to mend a hundred pieces with the Ega Pega . . . Maybe it is the little girl's making such a thing about her life that is causing Rosa to slip back into a habit she had as a teenager in love with Alejandro: making up little dream scenes . . . about Wolfie now that she never sees him. It is ridiculous. She even thinks up things he would say to her if he could talk. Sometimes she imagines it's Wolfie she's telling all these stories to, instead of the little girl. What made her think back then that he wouldn't have been interested in her life? When he was well, he helped a lot of people she knew with their problems: Dalila Flores whose husband was trying to work and take care of her four children that time the Migra wouldn't let her back in the country after she went to see her dying mother in Mexico. There wasn't any money in it for Wolfie, helping them; so he had to be interested in Dalila's problem.

Rosa's problem was her story. She could have told Wolfie her story while he was busying himself with her breasts.

And Lidia Bustamante's husband who built a garage without permits and the town was going to knock it down just like they did to the house Laureano was building in Jackson Township... Wolfie saved Lidia's garage, and he would have helped Rosa if she'd known him back then.

If they ever send her to him again, she'll tell him all her thoughts. He can't speak, but he can hear. What an idiot she was, never talking to him all those days. Only baby talk. How could she have...?

In the meantime she imagines him watching her from his wheelchair: not just at the Sunshine Club, where he might actually watch her, but everywhere: while she waits for Clifford to get into the bath, while she struggles to wash under Winnie's girdle. It makes her patient, and all her actions become somehow graceful and even beautiful, as if Wolfie is aware of them. It's absurd, she knows. How would he get himself in his heavy motorized wheelchair into hiding places to spy on her wherever she goes?

Sometimes, like today, when the dragging womb brings the memory rushing back, and she feels Wolfie's hands, feels the yearning for his lips on her breast, she goes into the bathroom and locks the door and fondles her own right breast and brings herself. Oh, Oh, Oh Wolfie...

And of course she is ashamed. She is a shameful person. She watches people around her: Priscilla, Mrs. Rose, Eulalie Arsenault, Mrs. Hingy at the agency, and she knows that none of them have such shameful thoughts as she, Rosa.

It was the Fahey woman told the agency, she's certain. On Monday, coming from the sisters' house, she sees her waiting for the bus with her big plastic *bolsa* where she carries her flip-flops and her sandwiches and her police radio, things she needs to be *comfy*, as she calls it, during an overnight. Once, when their shifts overlapped, Rosa caught her with her feet up, and her food spread out listening on that radio to all the neighborhood criminal activity, ignoring Eulalie's calls for a drink of water.

And she's the one goes to Wolfie now. Sooner kiss a mackerel than that woman, Alcide Arsenault observed to Rosa once.

So as to keep up her self-respect a little, Rosa needs to recall how Wolfie's caresses began, how apologetic he had been, and worshipful, not of Rosa but of some idea he had of woman.

Ooman. He got the word out one day as she bent to help him into his chair. He had his good hand on her waist, so he could feel where her hip swelled out. Rosa, like her mother, was *una mujer bien plantada*.

Woman. He ran his fingers over her hip, thinking some other words he couldn't say. He was almost like the midwife in Xoyatla, *misia* Fernanda, sizing up Mondo's approaching birth, was she wide enough?

All this was outside her clothes. Like a blind man figuring the shape of a once-familiar object. Another time she needed to bend over him to brush his hair, he weighed her right breast with his good hand and moaned. Then his eyes asked forgiveness, poor man; he suffered more than she did during this stage of his studying her. She couldn't help it, her right breast was wishing away the cloth of her blouse, her bra. Shameless woman. None of this is for Esmeralda's ears.

Sometimes, like a doctor or a priest, his eyes questioned her, as if he wanted her to explain to him what all this meant. Then her own thoughts hid themselves. How could she say what her breast desired?

And all this time, and even before, she saw him helpless and naked in the bath chair. As he stood holding her shoulders, she washed his thighs and buttocks and behind his scrotum, only handing him the washcloth, as she'd been instructed in the classes, for him to wash his own penis.

His body was beautiful to Rosa, his skin white and spotless like her aunt's gardenia blossoms. His affected legs gone back to a child's unmuscled body. In the chapel of the Italian church was a nearly naked Christ figure, laid across his mother's lap, that reminded Rosa of Wolfie. Wolfie was a Jew like Jesus, she knew, and she didn't believe what some said about the Jews killing Jesus. Why would they kill their own beautiful son? There had to be some other explanation.

Wolfie was painfully thin. Under the arch of his ribs his stomach was hollow, like the cave beneath the ribs of the crucified Jesus. To Rosa this was achingly sad. She was a student of crucifixes and had her own large plaster figure in her bedroom. She had bought it at a yard sale and felt rich in religious art since hanging it over the bed. Laureano called it the *estatua de la mala muerte* and accused it of coming into his dreams. To Rosa the great arch under the breastbone represented suffering: the strain of the raised arms supporting the weight of the body. She wondered if the little peg securing the feet to the post offered any relief. Probably it hurt too much to rest any weight on it. Usually the face, fallen over like a wilted flower, reflected patience or resignation; the pain was there in the great arch of the ribs and the hollow beneath.

Wolfie didn't eat enough to keep himself nourished and sometimes had to have a feeding tube. Rosa could coax him and make sure he ate while she was going to him. She was sure this wasn't the case anymore. Sometimes she would look over at his table at the Sunshine Club and note that the aides had put the tray beyond his reach or had not removed all the little lids on the bowls and cups.

What did his body look like now? she wondered. Did it require Rosa's attendance for its beauty?

She was guilty of taking more time about Wolfie's bath, for example, than she did with a man like Clifford. She had also studied him seriously, taking time to straighten his bad arm and flex the fingers, making sure to thoroughly wash inside the clenched palm.

You couldn't see the penis of the figure in the Italian church, but she thought it must be well-developed like Wolfie's. It was the largest penis she had ever seen. And the only Jewish one. She wasn't sure what this meant. Usually it nestled fatly in its nest of curly black hair between Wolfie's legs. A sleeping animal.

But sometimes, like her breast, it woke and had something it wanted; then they both looked at it with concern.

For a long time, in any case, Rosa knew his flesh, while her flesh could only wish the clothes away. If he wanted to know hers, he must advance on his own. She knew if he did she would not scream or put in a complaint as some of the aides had done. That was all she knew.

Then, when summer came, one day she wore a loose little chemise with slender shoulder straps and the bra built in, so that you didn't have two sets of straps. It was pretty and not the sort of thing she usually wore unless it was very hot out. He couldn't take his eyes off of it while she helped him undress for his bath; and once she got him seated on the bath chair the sleeping penis came out of its nest and stood up proudly. Rosa laughed, and they were comfortable enough together by then that he laughed too, and then into the loose chemise went his hand and found her bare nipple. She couldn't help gasping in pleasure.

Ooman, he groaned. Ooman! And then he found the flesh at her middle and her hip and her belly, and then he knew, dear man, that her breast was calling him back to the nipple; and that was enough to bring Rosa, so long she had been waiting.

So Rosa came to represent Woman to Wolfie, and he worshipped her and she accepted his worship.

But it was a sin, Rosa told herself. And now they were both punished. Rosa had taken up the study of sin when she used to teach the catechism classes to the little Mexican children at Saint Barnabas. There were little sins and big sins and if you committed too many little sins you were more likely to go on to the big ones. Some sins you did in your mind and then, sometimes, you went on to let yourself fall into them. This was the kind of sin she and Wolfie were doing. But Rosa never felt this quite covered the study of sin, and had her own thoughts about it.

Next day the bloodletting is worse. The labor pains, the clots passing. The last time wasn't so bad; it lasted a whole week, but it wasn't so much blood. This is the real thing: she has to call in and go to bed. The little girl comes over and fixes her some tea and toast. Does she get hers yet? Rosa wonders, as the girl stirs about in the kitchen. Probably not, but she will soon, by the looks of her. Already she looks like her mother, with her dark eyes under the heavy bang. A kind child. Rosa wishes her a happy life. She will be successful, like Eva.

Eva was kind, even when she was a baby. Rosa clung to her for comfort after she left Alejandro and went to her aunt's. Now she's in the Army in Georgia, but calls every week. Soon she'll be a colonel, Rosa thinks with a flush of pride.

I gave Don Laureano some too, the little girl tells her when she comes with a tray. A pretty one Eva gave her for Mother's Day—Rosa hung it on the wall and never thought to use it. And the toast arranged so pretty in triangles on the plate.

He really did build all those houses he tells you about, Rosa says, embarrassed for Laureano, who is soft in the head for the little girl.

Tell me about one of them. Well, the best of them was torn down. It have bathrooms and a pretty deck you can see the river from. The Shawsheen River. It was going to have a family room with a wood stove, and carpets all through.

And why did they tear it down? Town did it. He don't get the permits. He go to get them and they insult him, he says. So he build it without them. And before he can finish it they come and knock it over with a bulldozer.

Goodness!

He still have some of the materials, so he pay a contractor to get the permits and buy another lot in the township and put it up again, almost as nice.

Well, it was a long time ago. I remember it take me two buses then and a long walk to go to work in the apple packing... You are so clever to find that tray. My daughter give it to me. She is almost a colonel in the Army.

Yes, they send her to school, she's so smart. School for social work. When she gets out in fifteen years she have a house she save to buy and a career to work, plus her pension.

V.
Piety Corner

Next day she drags herself to Piety Corner, check on Helen Schade, woman who spent most of her life in Metropolitan State Hospital. Now she's inherited the big old mansion where her parents used to live on Lura Lane and lives there for spells between the hospital.

Straighten up the house and check she's eating, the agency tells her. She'd like to see *them* straighten up this place, she thinks, clearing a space so she can get into the foyer, her womb still dragging at her.

Once in, she encounters a new obstacle: a forest of entangled aluminum legs, crutches, walkers, commodes—stuff the old parents left behind. You suppose I can put these out to the trash? she calls into the kitchen, where Helen lives in a space cleared around the breakfast nook—she eats at the table, sleeps in the window seat on a bare dirty cushion.

DON'T THROW ANYTHING OUT!

Hokay, hokay. Just vacuum a little and straighten up, they told her at the agency. Well that's not possible, thinks Rosa. She'll follow, rather, her aunt's advice: a house is clean if the toilet, sinks, and refrigerator are clean. She starts in the bathroom, which takes the three hours she's allowed. You didn't throw anything out, Helen yells.

No, no. I'll just fill this wastebasket with some of those flyers messing up the floor there. There is a mountain of mail in the corner of the breakfast nook, from which small avalanches have toppled inward to cover half the floor. That's my mail. I need to sort through it.

Just the ads, I mean.

I might need them. I order things.

Oh, well, maybe I help you...

YOU ARE NOT TO THROW ANYTHING OUT!

Hokay. I throw only this dirty water outside.

Let me see it.

Rosa shows her the water. *Inmundo*, she thinks.

She takes the pail outside and down to the little stream at the bottom of the hill with a little wooden bridge to cross and throws the water into it. She admires a bed of withered lilies of the valley still sweetening the air and indulges in a little dream of bringing Wolfie here someday in his chair. She has a feeling Wolfie would appreciate Piety Corner with its old houses and big trees.

And let me see in your bag now, that you take nothing, she is told when she goes back in the house to get her things. This hasn't happened to Rosa since she first worked in the apple packing and Mr. Haffenhover used to check them as they left work. What he think they take? Apples? They saw too many apples to ever want one again.

She hands the bag to Helen. Someone is taking stuff out of this house, and I have to find out who it is, Helen says.

Rosa looks around at the subsiding stacks of supermarket flyers and Wal-Lex coupons, the upside-down furniture and clothing on rolling racks that look as if they come from a dress store...

My sister, I think it is. She was always jealous of me; now I got this house. She has a twenty-room house herself and three cars. Why does she have to come snooping around here when I'm gone?

You go out? Rosa asks. She looks so permanent there on her bench in the breakfast nook surrounded by coffee cups she won't let Rosa wash...

Of course I go out. I have my supermarket cart so I can take my most valuable things with me. Rosa used to see her downtown with her cart full of rags and blankets and an orange cat on top, but not lately.

Maybe I not go back, thinks Rosa, walking back down Lexington Street to the bus from Lexington, which is always full with her people, who work for the rich people there.

But the next week on Friday, following her aunt's rules of cleanliness—kitchens first, then bathrooms—she spends her three hours on the refrigerator. It is the most daunting of her tasks, and she had thought to leave it till last; but, like Mrs. Rose with her music, Rosa likes to do the hard parts first.

In the front are cartons of Chinese food, from the Celestial Mandarin at Wal-Lex Plaza. All of Helen's food seems to come from there. No wonder her legs are all swollen up. These all look fairly recent, and she has orders to not throw any of them out, so these she sets on a small space she finds on the floor without even looking inside. What is in back of them looks to have been in there for years, so long even the wax paper around some of them has decayed and has a fuzz all over: *inmundo*

inmundo. She scrapes it all out with a spatula into a plastic bag.

I need to know where is your garbage, she asks Helen, who is seated in her usual place with her swollen legs up.

I don't know where it is since I came here. I take it downtown to the dumpster behind the Cozy Kitchen when I need to.

Rosa stands up from where she's been kneeling on the filthy floor. Madre de Cristo! she hollers. I not taking this filth back downtown with me! I will find something!

She stalks outside with the pestilent bag and notes the neighbors have their cans out to the curb. She finds a half-empty one next door, where it looks like no one's home, and shoves the bag in. If Wolfie could see her now! Then she finds a large plastic bucket under the back porch and hauls in inside. This is your garbage, see! Today is Friday. It go out on Friday.

Well I hardly ever have anything. Rosa doesn't hear. She has her head inside the refrigerator scraping green fuzz, black fuzz, white fuzz, with a knife. The hard part first. She'll feel better after.

VI.
The Sunshine Club

It is Berta Bechtel's birthday at the Sunshine Club. Rosa wheels Winnie up to the Reality Orientation and goes to sit near Mrs. Rose, who has brought her harp today and is playing something Rosa has heard before. She recognizes a series of yearning passages aiming, it seems to her, at a certain immensely satisfying note, but avoiding it avoiding it. There it comes. It comes. The music is triumphant now, whirling around like a flock of sparrows and off with a final flourish. Rosa has never been teased like this before by a piece of music. What is the secret of it? She wishes she could ask Mrs. Rose about it, but how?

Mrs. Rose told Rosa once that her mother used to play piano pieces only up to the hard parts, then quit. When Mrs. Rose was a girl and wanted to study the violin, her mother told her only a harp was a ladylike instrument for a girl, so she studied the harp, but learned the hard parts first. Rosa is certain Mrs. Rose could answer any of her questions about music; but she, Rosa, just as certainly doesn't know how to ask them.

Rebecca brings a group into the kitchen, and Bobby Rosier is allowed to stick the candles in the cake. Meanwhile Berta goes to the piano and Priscilla accompanies her while she sings "Columbia the Gem of the Ocean." She's dressed in a green taffeta skirt with a little jacket with orange piping and holds a green patent leather pocketbook against her breast.

Lunch is served first, and Rosa mashes up the peas and potatoes to feed Winnie, who must be coaxed. Lately she will not touch any meat. Bobby Rosier is so excited about the cake in the kitchen he goes around whispering loudly to everyone that they mustn't tell Berta about it.

You're the only one talking about it, Bobby, says Terry Fratus acidly. Why don't you sit down and shut up?

Now, now, says Mrs. Rose. Let's not spoil this nice lunch. Nice lunch! says Terry. This patty here, what do you suppose is in it, some kind of cat food? Or maybe it's rabbit food. It has little specks of carrot in it.

Obstreperous, screeches Winnie, and Rosa slips a spoonful of red Jell-o into her gaping mouth.

My mother had a recipe once for some patties, says Isa Babcock. It called for spinach, and we used to go out in the fields to pick wild yarrow as a substitute. Isa, who wears one of two dresses every day, is descended from a founder of the city.

Lately, Rosa goes to Saturday Mass at Saint Anthony's, at five so she can sleep on Sunday. The Mexicans, as usual this time of year, are setting up the altar around a dressed-up doll to represent one of their Virgins. It's the Mexicans get all the attention here. So many of them. It's all their little songs they sing, their Virgin. We have a Virgin too in Honduras, Rosa thinks.

They have a new priest, a gringo, who seems to think he's speaking Spanish when he gives the homily. Hermanilla Vargas sitting across the aisle gives Rosa a look, and they smile behind their song sheets. The announcements are even more bewildering: there is to be a Bring Yourself in a Covered Pot Banquet and a Try To Be Proud of Your Relatives Discussion.

I enjoyed your sermon very much, Rosa says firmly in English as they file out.

After supper that night she goes into the kitchen to lock the back door just before she goes to bed and surprises a cockroach in the sink, second time that weekend. She'll call the extermination tomorrow. Before the Guatemalans she never had cockroaches.

VII. Eulalie Arsenault Is Dying

Eulalie Arsenault is dying. It seems like only weeks ago she was hiding Alcide's walker so he couldn't get away from her and complaining in her firm voice that he was im-po-seeb and going to Grover Cronin's and to choir practice. Now, either Rosa or Priscilla is there part of the day to tend to Alcide—the Fahey woman used to go, but the agency came one day and found she had tied Alcide to a chair. Hospice comes to tend to Eulalie.

She and Priscilla have taken to accompanying Alcide downtown while Eulalie sleeps, to tire him out so he'll take a long nap afterward and allow them time to fix his supper and do the wash. Usually her day falls on Thursday and she considers it her happy day, though it's sad to see Eulalie so brought down by her cancer, which is in her spine now.

Today he wants to go to the car lot, where they let him sit out front waving a sign that says SALE TODAY. He wears a tie for these occasions. Rosa sits inside with Cristos and Batty and sees they don't make fun of him or tire him too much. On the way back they lean over the railing of the Gold Star Mothers Bridge and watch the Styrofoam cups float among the pilings that used to hold up Nuttings Dance Hall, where Alcide tells her he used to bring a woman named Irish Peggy. You never bring Eulalie?

It was one of the bad places the teachers told her a nice woman should never go. She was very, how you say, *propaire*.

What teachers?

At the school. The English and Civics class. Rosa has heard this before, but enjoys Alcide's memories.

She wouldn't even let me kiss her until she had a ring on her finger.

So what you do together?

Well, kitchen rackets. After she got the ring.

What is they?

Well, the Irish. They were as strict as the French. In the kitchens. They had bands. Fiddles, and spoons, even pots and pans. Sometimes we danced, if there was room. Or we just stamped around. Showed off our uniforms, and the girls' new dresses. Eulalie sewed her dresses.

Was she pretty then?

She was a beauty. The best of all the girls. The smallest waist, the sweetest hips, My Eulalie…

When she went down to the basement to collect the rent on Friday—Laureano made her do this—there was no one home. She looked in all the rooms, finally found little Beatrice with her new baby in a dark back bedroom under the covers.

Qué pasa? *La migración.* They went out the back window. Rosa notes the two back windows with a chair underneath, open and the screens broken out. When?

This morning. At breakfast. Rosa doesn't believe it about the *migración*. They never came to houses. You couldn't see from outside if a house had roomers, or there was an apartment downstairs. She went down at ten and found Eusebio, the oldest tenant.

What did they say?

Algo como migration.

Fumigation?

Something like that, like migration.

Fumigation?

Maybe, maybe. We get scared.

FUMIGATION!

Maybe…

I *called* them. The cockroaches. *Idiotas.*

VIII.
A Goat

Laureano comes home with a goat on a leash. He ties it to a concrete block and lets it crop the side lawn. It's a billy and Rosa won't go near it.

What about the Animal Control? The only animals we can have are dogs and cats.

You and your dogs and cats. There's no profit in them. This *chivo* we're going to roast next month.

After the animal has cropped the side lawn, Laureano drags the concrete block to the rear and then around the other side. He eats all her rose bushes and the hosta she'd planted around the fruit trees. All the same Rosa has become quite fond of him and buys him apples. After all her years packing apples, Rosa thinks they are only a treat for goats. She asks Laureano if they might buy a female and breed him. There is nothing in the world as tender as a baby goat. He surprises her and comes home with a female. The two of them are tethered to two concrete blocks now, so they can't get around front and be seen. We'll roast the baby! he says.

No, no, the baby is mine. You can roast the billy.

Sentimental old woman, he says. And he's all of twenty years older than she is.

The tenants have returned, one by one late at night. Rosa makes the lazy girl in bed with her baby all day get up and clean the place. Then she calls the fumigation again.

Idiotas.

Guatemalans.

IX.
Gina

She has a new consumer. That's what you're supposed to call them now. Before it was clients, and before that they were patients. What will it be next?

The woman, who lives out in Piety Corner near Helen Schade, speaks no English.

She has just been brought from Italy by her daughter, who is a doctor and must leave her alone all day. When Rosa arrives she is weeping and scrubbing the kitchen table, which is already clean.

Rosa, not knowing what else to do, goes and puts her arms around her. The woman, whose name is Gina, begins to tell Rosa in Italian about her only son who died recently in Turin, leaving her all alone, with just this daughter who works all day. And there is not even a store she can walk to or a neighbor who is home.

Rosa is supposed to be cleaning the house, which she can see is spotless, so she just puts on some water to boil for coffee and seats the woman at the kitchen table beside her and holds her both hands in hers. Gradually she becomes aware that a great deal of what the poor lady is saying, she is understanding.

Quiere café? she tries out.

Sí, sí.
Dónde está?
Dove e . . .
Sí, sí.

Del Mediterranio. Gina points to herself and then to Rosa. Then gets up to find the coffee and a little cast aluminum espresso pot with rubber rings where you screw it together, fills the top with powdery coffee and pours the boiling water into it.

Rosa watches. She remembers seeing pots like this in corner stores in Xoyatla. The milk hot, she understands next. *La leche caliente . . .* Two Mediterranean ladies, Gina insists. Rosa doesn't get this about the Mediterranean. But at home they always scalded the milk. She still does it.

Now they're both rushing around the kitchen. They find the milk and put it to heat. Her daughter's terribly weak coffee with cold milk in it was disgusting, Rosa understands.

Sí, sí, sin gusto, sin sabor . . . They embrace. Two Mediteranean ladies, two ladies who understand the right way to drink coffee. Yes, they congratulate each other.

Delicioso, she says, sipping the cup that Gina has half filled with the strong brew and the boiled milk.

Sí, Sí!

Rosa picks the thin film off the surface. *La nata*, she says. Gina shakes her head, puzzled, then laughs, and they embrace again.

So the day goes. There is nothing to clean. The house has gleaming wood floors and pure white walls with large paintings of nothing in pretty colors, and a few very old paintings in dark glowing colors: faces and views. She is shown three neat bedrooms and a dustless library; and there is the cat who has come all the way from Torino, Italy, a beautiful creature asleep on a lacy pillow on Gina's bed. *Bello, bello.* There are dresses to look at, and shawls she has made herself.

Then Gina makes her sit and brings her crocheting, her sewing projects to the dining room table to display. *Bello, bello.*

At noon they have a little lunch Gina has prepared already, a fragrant soup of tiny dumplings and spinach and a fish salad she has ready for her daughter's supper, which they must sample. Rosa begins to protest about how she needs to help, to cook, to clean; *cocinar, limpiar*... but Gina firmly misunderstands all these words.

After the lunch, Gina puts the dishes in the dishwasher, and Rosa watches to see how it's done. Then she watches Gina clean the two bird cages in a pretty sun-room off of the large kitchen, and fill the little feeders with seeds. There is a white cockatiel and a small green parrot living with a lime colored parakeet named Domenico, who is Gina's favorite and gives kisses.

The crocheting is brought out again. The hours drag on. Finally it is three o'clock and Gina takes some deeply chocolate bars out of the oven, and the two Mediterranean ladies heat some more milk to color with the strong brew in the cast aluminum pot, and there is another self-congratulatory sitting down to tiny cups of *latte* in which they dip the little finger-shaped biscuits. Rosa thinks she learns from Gina that she had only two children, that her son died of a blood disease, that her husband died many years before, and that he had been a singer of opera.

After she gets home, Rosa calls to inform the agency of this bewildering state of affairs and is told that the doctor daughter is thrilled with the arrangement. Rosa is to do an extra day each week and do exactly as Gina expects her to. We didn't know you spoke Italian, they tell her.

I don't speak Italian. Well, they think you're from Spain, which is almost the same as Italy. Rosa looks at an atlas Laureano sent away for and finds Spain—a place as remote from her as China. When little Esmeralda comes they find Italy and Torino, and the Mediterranean Sea, so that now Rosa understands what is meant by Two Mediterranean Ladies who like their milk heated for their coffee.

This is the stuff of dreams, in Rosa's opinion. Like her fantasies about Wolfie. It is many weeks before she is even halfway used to the arrangement. Her body itches to rise from the breakfast table and run the vacuum. She even has to remain sitting while Gina washes the breakfast dishes. Some of the food she is served is delicious, and other things are strange and tasteless. It is almost more of an ordeal than a pleasure, carrying out some of these obligations; she can't explain it. Finally, she picks up some of the embroidery Gina is working on and says: *Enseñarme. Demostrarme.*

So the next time Rosa comes, there is a new piece of cloth with a basket of flowers printed on it that the doctor daughter had picked up especially for Rosa. She follows Gina in making the centers and the petals of the flowers, and this helps her to sit still at least, as the dainties are set before her.

Ever since the little girl came to interview her Rosa's life has taken this novel turn. One day on Moody Street a woman stops her to tell her she has the nicest smile on her face. Another day on Main Street she practically walks into the arms of the Kisser, something she's managed to avoid for years.

He is wearing his admiral's uniform today and fairly clean and sweet smelling. His kiss is soft and his eyelashes flutter against her temple. Not a dirty kiss, Rosa used to tell people who were afraid of him. Like a brother kiss a sister. They both smile after the kiss, then Rosa laughs. Here she is going about dreaming of shameful things and she's been caught. Serves her right!

X.
October Coming On

The billy has mounted the female goat, and she is becoming fat. Rosa feeds her pears and apples and leftover coffee cake. She's taken a folding chair out to where they are tied, and the nanny nuzzles in her lap like one of the tabby cats. As the creature's belly swells, Rosa feels the engorging in her own belly. The billy is an indifferent animal who has discovered he can drag his concrete blocks all the way around the house, so a second block must be added. Rosa won't mind eating him. She walks along the river, not to catch the bus today; it is Sunday after church, the day Esmeralda's mother makes tamales. Rosa goes to the Mexican store to buy Laureano the mole tamales he loves.

All the berries out today along the river. Purple gooseberry, red box, cloudy blue juniper, and flaming bittersweet. And the wind blowing every which way so there are no clouds in the choppy water. Only in their proper place above, Rosa notes. The little waves break over the pebbles, and the marsh grasses stand on their legs in the tea-colored water.

I no see my heron anymore because of you silly clown hats, she tells Don Amable behind the counter, and he laughs. They can find somewhere else to drop their shit, he says with satisfaction. Esmeralda brings out four of her mother's tamales wrapped in corn husks. In her country they wrap them in plantain leaves. She will come to ask Rosa more questions on Tuesday afternoon, the little girl tells her.

Walking back, Rosa wonders if there is anything more left in her life that she can properly tell a ten-year-old. They would have to be things she hadn't even told her own children.

Winter is settling in. There are frosts and snow squalls. Then a rare snowstorm in November. Rosa walks out to Piety Corner now for Helen's Tuesdays and Gina's Monday and Fridays after Clifford's bath. She must take the bus back to be at Eulalie's on time.

She is a good walker. When they lived in Billerica she had to walk seven miles both ways to the orchards. There was no bus. When Rosa walks she keeps her body leaned forward, her legs moving swiftly, her eyes on the ground. This was the way women walked in Xoyatla, behind their husbands, carrying sticks for cooking fires on their heads. This was the way she walked in Xoyatla, on narrow trails, where roots and stones could trip you, bringing her father his lunch in two interlocking aluminum pails, hurrying home to rinse out the sheets and towels stretched in the sun on the banks of the river; later, then, bringing Alejandro his lunches, hurrying home to the babies. A road never looked trackless to Rosa. Head down, she recognized a flat stone where the road began to climb, a stand of guadua that marked a turn to the left that meant you were nearing the village. Once, long ago, before her aunt, before she was expected to work, she used to wander in the woods imagining a large palace. Clearings were rooms with moss for carpets and stones were seats and logs were divans or banquet tables. During her mother's sickness she came to her favorite of these rooms and thought how she could come here to live if necessary. There was a soft bed of moss to sleep on, and blackberries to eat nearby and the long phalluses of plantain overhanging and the coffee bushes beneath, whose berries she picked and munched.

Now Rosa walks on the verge of Lexington Road and notes weeds that seem to her more beautiful than some of the plants for sale outside the Waltham Supermarket. Who decides what's a weed and what you must put in your garden? she wonders. She sees a single glove and thinks about its mate, its owner . . . An unreeled cassette tape. A crushed ballpoint showing its innards. A deflated condom. Sometimes there is something she can use: a red scarf, a ski hat. And blackberries, just like the *moras* at home. Walking was unlike riding a bus. You saw things on the ground; you wondered about them. On a bus you saw people and wondered; you looked into the windows of houses and wondered, What if I lived there?

She knew later, much later, that her mother died of womb cancer. At the time she and her sisters assumed she died of their laziness, their failure to help her. That was the impression their father gave them, that they could have saved her if they'd tried harder.

Tito, who was the last to come from her womb, believed he had killed her. Long after the sisters had half forgiven themselves, Tito still believed he had killed his mother.

When Rosa first came to Lowell and lived in a back room of Tito's apartment, he told her this. Her older sister Gloria Helena, who came next and then moved to Chicago, told Rosa that the cancer was in her womb before Tito was conceived. She never told Tito this because, soon after she came, he took his growing family to Miami, and she could never afford to visit.

There had been a lot of blood during her mother's illness. A lot of bloody sheets soaking in bleach or stretched in the sun on the bank of the stream behind their house they washed in this stream; it was too small to have a name so they called it *el sin nombre*; while the river at the bottom of the mountain was the Plata.

Only briefly will Rosa allow her thoughts to rest on that blood and her own bloody monthly. Cancer was something you couldn't think much about. And besides, she felt strong, stronger than cancer. She knew there was no cancer in her womb when she carried Eva.

She'd have liked to have a child with Laureano, even though he considers he has enough children by the woman, Yvonne, who left him in 1970 with twins and a daughter to bring up. She still hopes it might happen, even though she is coming close to fifty. If the Virgin wants this to happen it will happen, she believes. The children of the woman, Yvonne—who everybody in the neighborhood seems to despise, except for the next door neighbor Mrs. Connor—have not turned out all that well; but Laureano indulges them, giving them money for their schemes and hoping each time they'll put it to some better use than buying drugs and rum.

One of Rosa's most shameful thoughts is of having a child by Wolfie. Back when she was going to him regularly she daydreamed of the admittedly impossible idea that she had met Wolfie before his stroke. Of course she wouldn't have been his wife, rather a woman on the side, a mistress; though Wolfie didn't seem the type to have a mistress. Jews, she thought, probably didn't have mistresses. Anyway she dismissed all the difficulties and imagined the child. White, he would be. As beautifully white as Mondo was brown. Wolfie is white, almost blue in his whiteness, Rosa thinks. His whiteness would overcome her darkness. And studious. Intelligent as Mondo and Laureano, but studious too. He would want to be a lawyer like his father. The notion of being a street artist like Mondo, or any such other notion, would be gently discouraged by his father. By his father, who would consider him in every way his son, who would love him in secret as much as his other two sons. As he loved the mother, whose story moved him, whose problems interested him.

Ah, Wolfie. She also indulged a fantasy of the post-stroke, present Wolfie fathering a son with her, Rosa.

One day, maybe two years ago, he conveyed to her a desire to do it with her not in the bath chair with her sitting on the edge of the tub, but on the bed. So, before his bath, she lifted him from his chair onto the bed she had just made up and laid him down and pulled down his pajama pants. Then she let him open her blouse and helped him take down her panties; and lay down beside him. On top, on top he signaled somehow, so she lay on top, but this hindered his movement so she rolled off and began caressing his penis and his dark nipples until he was standing up hard and purple, and deep groans were coming from his throat. So she then tried again to get atop him kneeling above him and almost, almost succeeding in getting him inside her before he lost enough of his hardness to prevent getting all the way in. This was awkward, and she was far from aroused herself. So, feeling rather embarrassed and sluttish now in the early morning light on his narrow hospital bed, she finished by kneeling above his penis and sucking him till he came.

It could have worked, she thinks now, with a little more practice, but he must have felt awkward too and never asked for it again.

If they try again, she will have to take the lead and come to him at night in his bed. She will be quicker and more agile. She knows she can do it. And he will feel more of a man. How proud he will be, going down to the Sunshine Club after, dressed in shirt and tie, his beautiful dark hair combed over his brow in the most becoming way only Rosa knows to comb it, a man who has had his way with a woman.

XI.
Wolfie across the Room

Winnie isn't eating well, so either Rosa or Priscilla must stay with her at the Sunshine Club through lunch to see she eats. On days that Rosa is there, she sometimes sees Wolfie across the room. He has a little keyboard now attached to his wheelchair. Rebecca can read what he writes on the screen above. Mostly it is simple requests already spelled out on one key: like "bathroom," or "drink of water," that he can punch in, Rebecca says. There are also single letters like on a typewriter, and maybe with practice he can learn to write his own sentences, Priscilla says when Rosa questions her. She thinks one of his sons got it for him.

Rosa speculates on this. Could it happen that Wolfie could write to someone about what the Fahey woman does when she is alone with him? How she is careless and cruel with him as Rosa knows she is with others who can't complain.

Now her daydreams include this new device. He will learn to write. He will write,

HELP,

like the headboard of the bus that got lost with Henrietta Rose aboard, that driver who was Bemis and thought he was Kenmore, and, fumbling with the headboard, turned it to

HELP

while police from two towns were chasing him.

HELP,

Wolfie will write, and someone will see it, maybe his son. Maybe the son is a good man, like Wolfie, so he will want to know more, and he will investigate and the Fahey woman will be caught. They will find her with her feet up and her teeth out, gumming her sandwiches and listening to her police radio while some helpless client is calling. And then—Rosa hardly dares think this—he will write,

ROSA.

Could it be? And then the son will tell the agency—like Gina's doctor daughter—that Rosa must do exactly as the client . . . the consumer . . . wishes. And in this case, Rosa will not sit trapped at a table, feeding Winnie, or held at another table being served by Gina and working tiny embroidered flowers, but will run here and there pleasing Wolfie and talking to him so that he can answer and tell her everything on his new little machine, words of love and gratitude to match her own.

Ah, Rosa, these are her thoughts as she walks the verge of Lexington Road to Piety Corner.

XII.
A Pretty Envelope

A pretty envelope arrives in the mail. Rosa is mystified, even after opening it. A thank you note signed,

Dr. Eugenia Garofalo.

She reads the note, uncomprehending . . .

. . . that my mother should encounter a Spanish lady able to communicate with her has alleviated a burden I took on in bringing her here to a strange place. Much as I love her I cannot stay home with her every day . . .

Spanish lady? It is evening before she understands. It is the doctor daughter. As Rosa has noted, Spain is as foreign to her as China. As she is clearing away from supper and Laureano is watching Nova, Esmeralda knocks on the doorjamb and comes in the open kitchen door. Rosa sits her down at the table and puts on the kettle for the *manzanilla* infusion they drink evenings. Her ignorance about Spain, which would never have bothered her in the past, prompts her to ask the little girl why someone would assume that she, Rosa, is Spanish.

We speak Spanish. That is the language of Spain. Explorers came from Spain to our countries where we are from and became our ancestors.

I'm sure they aren't my ancestors, speaks Rosa. Well, not ours, but some of the people, and they made us forget our language and speak theirs.

Ours was no good.

No, I learned in school. Ours was a wonderful civilization. We had cities and roads and running water, and calendars and writing. They defeated us. No one knows why.

Ah. Rosa feels the old sadness of Xoyatla. The defeat. And Laureano. He was almost as dark as she, but long-faced; his long narrow nose, it must come from Spain. It was part of his ascendance over her, his ancestors. She had met his gray-eyed, long-faced mother years ago. And here he is with them, wanting to share their tea. Esmeralda gets up and pertly brings him a cup and puts the sugar in for him. She has him enraptured. She has chosen to pamper him. Laureano is an intelligent man. He watches programs on science and history on the TV. He reads a lot; but, because she pays attention at the school, Esmeralda knows as much as he, maybe more. How did you two meet? she asks, taking out her notebook.

Hah! Erupts Laureano. She thought she could walk here from Billerica. If I hadn't picked her up she would still be walking. I walked farther than that in my day, she says.

I looked at her sitting beside me in my cab, and I thought, *puro tribu*. Plenty more like her. But there was something . . . this neat little pair of legs that never quit.

Necio, says Rosa. I am thinking I be better off walking.

It was twenty-five miles.

So . . . could save myself a lot of trouble to come. The little girl's pertness is transferring itself to Rosa.

PART TWO

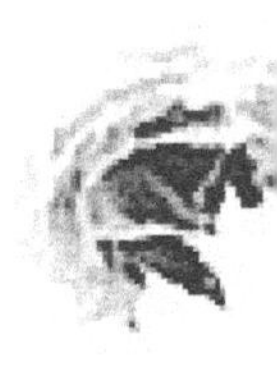

I.

Rosa Swears

It's to the point she almost doesn't recognize herself. And Tuesday, she swore openly at Helen Schade, told her if she doesn't want to put the trash out for the truck, then she must take the load downtown in her shopping cart right then, and Rosa was going to wash the dishes while she was gone and that was that.

Rosa was actually able to push her out the door with the kitty cat on top of her pile of trash.

She is getting smart is what it is, she thinks, soaping a sink full of cups and ashtrays and wiping down the kitchen counters and the table.

Laureano is smart, she thinks; because of all the TV he watches—Nova, the History Channel. Even he could have explained to her about Spain if she'd asked him. Eva is smart, because of her college education. A colonel. Rosa imagines all the ranks under her that Eva can order around. The little girl is smart because she pays attention to her teacher. Wolfie is smart because he …

She thinks now how she will be different if she can see him again, how she will tell him things and he will teach her things he knows with his new word machine.

And the little girl Esmeralda will teach her interesting things she can tell Wolfie about, like the great empire with the roads and the irrigation and the temples and the pyramids with stories carved into its walls, which Esmeralda showed her a picture of in her social studies book.

II.

Two Stories She Can't Tell Esmeralda

One of the stories she can't tell Esmeralda is the time ... it was before the time she really ran away to her aunt—and stayed there—when she ran to Alejandro's mother. It was a long time coming after the day he first pushed her, and it started when she was first pregnant with Eva. The somnolence came on her. She felt cold all the time and all she wanted to do was stand over the soup as it simmered on the wood stove, and drowse, wrapped in her poncho; or, after the wash was done, and the rice cooked and Mondo bathed, to go in the dark back bedroom and cover herself with the wool blankets and sleep. He caught her like this a couple times and the insults started. She was lazy; she was dreaming all the time; who was she dreaming of? The man who brought the milk in a pail every morning? She was a lazy whore.

Didn't he see the work was all done? Where was the tenderness he had showed her while she waited for Mondo to swell her belly? Probably the child was not his, he started to say. It was probably a girl this time. He didn't want a girl. Already he was forcing little Mondo to hold the measuring tape while he marked off where he would cut his frame for the new stable, to practice hammering a nail straight—impossible for a child who had just learned to walk.

"¡*Puta*!" The ugly word was spit out for the first time. She couldn't protest. It was too absurd and she was too sleepy.

Then there was the business that the house was his, he had built it, and she should leave, leave Mondo for him and go away.

Go away where? She could hardly believe this turn of events, but the leaving Mondo part was what scared her. Even though she could tell herself that it was just drunken raving, after he had come home and had his rice and beans and the meat from the soup that was only for him, and taken up his bottle of aguardiente seriously after sundown, she could tell herself that in the morning it would be forgotten. She took to keeping Mondo close all the time, hugging him to her in the bed at night. Then it was that she would make a *maricón* of him, a mama's boy, ruin him.

The child in her belly was not his, he ranted. Rosa, silent, wanted to say, Then whose could it be? The boy who brought the milk had twenty houses to service. Alejandro, it was, who would not keep a cow like most people. Too much work, he said. Who else did she see in her days? Her aunt, her neighbor who had no man . . .

Everybody knows you sleep with your uncle, he growled. This was truly shocking. Her uncle had tried to touch her once when she was still a girl and she had made so much noise, he had chosen her sister Yolanda over her, she suspected. Ever after he called her *La Escandalosa*, and never came near her.

Then one night, Alejandro's anger was menacingly silent. That was the first time he put her out of the house and slammed the door, not even putting in the bar. She simply waited an hour and snuck back in while he was asleep.

The next time, he did slide the bar in, and she had to spend the night, wrapped in her blanket, under the window where little Mondo slept, as if to protect him in some way, for Alejandro's last words to her were that this man child was his and she should take her bastard girl and go to her uncle. She remembers peeking in at the sleeping boy and recalling the day she lay in the hammock, watching Alejandro setting in this window, admiring the trueness of his corners, the expertness of his work.

It was all so ridiculous that she could almost have laughed. But it got worse. No matter for laughing.

She doesn't remember how many times she slept and woke out there before what she recalls as her long journey.

At the beginning, Alejandro seemed to sleep away his drunkenness and wake with no memory of his deeds of the night before. She had to pound on the door and he would let her in and fall back in bed while she started up the stove and made the coffee.

Sometime during her nights out there she did take note of a short ladder he had left in the back shed he was building, and began to make plans to get in the window at the boy's room.

By that time, all she could think about was Mondo. Not that his father would hurt him; he hadn't hurt her yet. What she was afraid of was that, in his stupor, he would forget to feed him, or that the child would go near the stove with no one watching him.

Some nights she was out, some she was in. Sometimes the door was barred, sometimes not. She found she could use the short ladder and climb in a kitchen window and sleep the rest of the night in the crib with Mondo. As long as the drunkard's sleep was undisturbed, these strategies worked, but there came the nights the drunk rose from the bed in the middle of the night and stalked like a zombie around the rooms. Sometimes he would fall and sleep where he lay, others, the wanderings went on till morning. She would come in the unbarred door or the window to find him sitting at the kitchen table waiting for his coffee and ready to continue the previous evening's fight.

This was the worst. The anger wasn't forgotten. It could begin again in the morning with ugly disjointed words. Mondo was beginning to say words, and the words were: *puta, carajo, la putamadre de la mala muerte*... these words would go on till late in the morning when Alejandro, instead of going out to work on the shed that would hold the pig, would fall into bed or on the floor and sleep for five or six hours and finally awake to begin the fight all over again.

They weren't really fights anymore. Rosa had stopped responding. Her silence made him angrier. *Muda! No tiene lengua? Se ve que es culpable.* Her silence confirmed her guilt.

She had thought of running to her aunt finally; but this would just convince Alejandro even more that the child in her belly was her uncle's.

But she knew now, she must run somewhere. And she had begun to prepare, hiding little packets of Mondo's clothing, blankets, powdered milk, and dry biscuits in the bushes; checking the hours of the bus that ran between Xoyatla and the port twice a day. The small ladder, which she always tried to return to its place in the shed after she had used it the night before to get in the kitchen window, she kept ready to use. The bedroom windows were too high to reach with it and Alejandro usually remembered to bar them at night.

It was possible to run away in the daytime, but she was afraid he would come after them. Usually he was fairly sober until evening; and also he kept Mondo about him, holding planks steady and receiving lessons on sawing and hammering from his father. This meant she would have to probably wait until evening or after midnight. The bus would have left by five o'clock, so she would have to walk till morning. Better to leave after midnight, walk a few hours, and catch the early morning bus.

And that was how it happened. It was a night when he barred the kitchen window but forgot the door, so she didn't need the little ladder. And, fortunately, it was a night he didn't take Mondo with him into the big bed. He was sick and restless, wandering, cursing, from room to room; then he found her hiding in the corner by the stove, and pulled her out into the middle of the room.

The boy stays and you go. She was foolish enough to argue: And how you take care of him? You no good for anything after the sun goes down.

He goes near the stove, you don't watch him. Maybe you forget to even give him his milk . . .

I don't forget. You forget. You sleep. She only sleeps when the child sleeps, she wanted to say, but knew better than to go into this further. She stood silent before the door. The child was whimpering in his room.

Puta! Desgraciada!

She said nothing.

Muda! Why doesn't she answer? She can't answer because I say the truth. Isn't it so?

La Muda. That's what he called her. The Mute One. Her silences enraged him.

She had no words. He came closer.

Isn't it so?

She shivered. The room was cold and the stove was out.

Isn't it true?

Yes, she said. Yes, don't…

And he punched the side of her head and put a fist into the pit of her stomach that caused her to lose her breath and double over, a darkness before her eyes.

She sat on the floor for a long while, trying to overcome nausea, to catch her breath.

Finally she was restored enough to note that the child was standing over her. He had figured out that he could roll his little mattress back and take out three of the wooden slats and crawl out beneath the crib. Mondo began outsmarting people before he was a year. There had never been a way of containing him.

Mama…

Mi amorcito.

They cried a bit together, then Rosa was all business.

Where was Alejandro?

She found him on the floor beside the bed, passed out, his cheek in a puddle of vomit.

She must leave. The only timepiece in the house was on Alejandro's wrist; she wouldn't take a chance of waking him. Possibly it was near dawn. In any case she must walk.

She must walk. She would go to Alejandro's mother, to Doña Merceditas. This decision she must have made beforehand, though she never said it to herself. If it were just herself to save she would have taken any of the mountain trails to another village. But there was Mondo. She could not go to her aunt, because of Alejandro's accusations. There was only the road. The road went to the little port at Aquadas, passing through Alejandro's village. A bus would come by just after dawn. In the meantime she must get away, she must walk.

There was a half moon. Mondo trotted along beside her with a little pack on his back carrying his bottle of Leche Klim sweetened with *panela*. Mondo was weaned, but when she knew she must leave, she had tried to get her milk back, taking him to her breast. It didn't come, of course, she was already pregnant. In a blanket sling over her shoulder were a few clothes, shoes, some crackers and cheese, and a little bit of money she had stolen from Alejandro's pocket. When Mondo put his arms around her leg and cried she lifted him into the sling and gave him the bottle to hold.

The sky was still dark, and clouds covered the moon. She stayed on the road mainly by the feel of it under her feet, and the branches that brushed by on her right side. The sleeping child was heavy and she had to keep adjusting the sling to ease first one shoulder, then the other. She lifted her feet high to avoid tripping, but couldn't avoid twice slipping down into the little channel beside the road and landing hard on her hip.

Mama puta, said Mondo awakening after the second fall, and she couldn't keep from bawling over this as she walked along. Poor little man, didn't know what he was saying, and yet it hurt her. Bawling, bawling, she came finally to the little *abasto* at a turn in the road, and there was a light in the front window. Someone up to start the stove? It would have been nice to go in and ask for some milky coffee, but all the money she had was for the bus. Also she knew it started before the first light, and what if she missed it for sitting down inside?

The road turned left and up just past the little store, she felt it with her feet. A hard climb, she tried to put little Mondo on his feet for a bit, but he was too tired and she had to pick him up again. If she could only see some other stove fires kindling. The sky was muffled in clouds and there were a few drops of rain. Help me, she moaned, help me Mother Mary. She felt she must walk at least a ways more to prevent Alejandro from catching her, but the blackness came before her eyes again and she found herself sitting in the road and sound asleep for a few moments until the boy kicked her awake and a pale light showed her where she was. The Virgin had brought the light and gently lifted her, for she was on her way again feeling the road more surely, and the child a bit lighter. In darkness she came to the top of the long hill. A false dawn. There was still no light in the sky or fires kindling, but the Virgin whispered that she had come far enough to be safe and must wait here for the bus. She could rest, but not sleep, the light inside her kept her from sleeping.

Feeling with her hands, she found a grassy hummock and sat, composing herself; so that when she heard the bus cough and grind its gears at the foot of the hill she had just climbed, she could stand and present herself as a woman, hair in place, blanket tightly wrapped, going to market. She was startled to see the bus driver was one of Alejandro's nephews, but he took her money without recognizing her and she had her choice of empty benches to sit on and organize her belongings around her. The buses in those days were wooden bodies on Ford truck chassis with open sides and long wooden benches.

Then she let herself doze without fear. When she woke there was a long streak of light dividing the darkness and a woman was nudging her: *Que te pasa? Tienes la boca toda sangre …*

Rosa put her hand to her mouth and wiped blood. A side tooth was loose and her cheek was cut on the inside. She moved the tooth with her tongue and it came out in her hand. Another woman handed her a napkin and she cleaned herself up as best she could. She shook her head at their questions: What happened? Did he beat you?

And she shut her eyes against the sideways sunlight coming in the front of the bus and the curious faces of these early market-goers, wanting to preserve the darkness around her, the light inside her, the deep rest the nagging sunlight was trying to pull her from.

Now Mondo was stirring. She opened her eyes and looked at the tooth in her hand. It marked the first loss of her fresh loveliness that had attracted Alejandro. He had first given her the sense of it; now he was taking it from her.

Mondo was crying. She tried to give him a cracker, but he pushed it back. He must have been thirsty, but she had no drink to offer. He was all sweaty when she unwrapped him from the blanket that had protected him from the chill mountain where they had caught the bus, which was now bucking its way downward toward the sea. She knew it stopped a couple of times before Alejandro's village. In her alarm she had given the driver too much money when she saw who he was, and had not waited for the change. But fortunately she still had a fifty-centavo piece in her bra. Maybe someone at the stop would give her a bit of juice in Mondo's empty bottle. Soon, soon, she crooned to him, allowing him to stand on the seat beside her and look around.

He was so beautiful, her honey-colored boy. And so ahead of himself. Before a year he was walking and talking. She was taking him to his grandmother Merceditas, who had many other grandchildren, but she must see this one is special.

The curious had been rebuffed by her in her shock at waking, but now Mondo was making friends among them. One handed him a slice of mango. The bus was now filled with daylight, too bright for the Virgin to remain with her. She was in Alejandro's place of sunshine and drowsing fishermen and singing and shouting. She turned to look behind her. Thank you, she said to them. I had a shock, she explained. Of course, they understood, they nodded. We know about these men, the woman directly behind her said.

At La Gorda, where they stopped, the woman told Rosa, You go in the market and wash your face. I will take the boy.

This kindness caused Rosa to cry for a while as they bumped along with the sparkling sea just beside the road. Then she took off Mondo's little shirt and soaked diaper and left him naked to cool off.

The bus pulled around a gas station and stopped at a little store. She took a fresh diaper out of her bundle and fastened it on Mondo and handed him back to the nice lady. "He can walk, you can put him down. Eight months and he can walk and call his mama *puta*, just like his papa."

Sin vergüenza, said the woman. You grow up to take care of your mama, she tells Mondo. Such a smart boy, he won't go punching a good woman like his mother, she said, bouncing the boy on her lap.

Rosa got off and went into the back of the little store, where there was the usual hole with the two steel footprints to stand on. She relieved herself gratefully, holding her breath against the odor. Just outside was a dirty sink where she wet one of Mondo's clean diapers and thoroughly washed her face, looking in a broken mirror. There was a darkening bruise on her cheek, but the missing tooth was only visible if she smiled widely, she noted. From that day on she was careful about how she smiled.

Then, with her last coin, she bought an orangeade for the nice woman. When would she ever touch money again? she wondered. Doña Merceditas surely wasn't going to give her any.

When she got back on the bus, she was as ready as she could be to present herself to Mondo's grandmamma.

No one answered her knock at the front of the pink-painted cement block house just off the little plaza. She went around the back where she found some young girls washing in the little stream behind the house. She be right back, a girl told her. There were many small children playing in the water, and Mondo pulled off his diaper and went to splash with them.

Rosa sat on a stone to wait, and let the water cool her dusty feet. Suppose she says no, go back to your man? Many older women said that. But there were a couple daughters-in-law already staying in the house. More likely she would say there is no room. Why you don't go to your own people? Rosa knew they found her shy and silent.

In that case, she decided to ask them to keep Mondo. They couldn't say no to their own blood. Then she would go to the big weekend houses up on the hill and work in one of them.

In the back of her mind, if Rosa could have admitted it, was the thought that Alejandro would guess where she was and would sober up and come after her.

Doña Merceditas finally came in a taxi with market baskets. There were so many thoughts and worries in Rosa's head by then that she could barely explain her presence. Merceditas, meanwhile, was so concerned with emptying her baskets and putting away the roots and greens she had bought, and seeing that the noon meal was put on the long table in the patio, that Rosa and Mondo were simply absorbed in the crowd of children and daughters-in-law as if they had been there for years.

Later, when the children and mothers were sleeping through the hottest hours of the afternoon and the wash lay stretched over the patio walls, Rosa found Merceditas sitting in the leatherette chair in the parlor, smoking her one cigarette she allowed herself a day, and said to her, simply, that she was grateful and that she would work hard, even find an outside job if she could. He hit me, Rosa said, touching her cheek.

So I see, said Merceditas. Nothing more was said. Rosa hung a hammock under the kitchen overhanging roof; and Mondo, her honey-colored boy, became indistinguishable in the naked troop of infants who played all day by the side of the creek and fell in a heap when night fell at the foot of Merceditas's double bed.

The sisters-in-law, Gomersinda and Marilena, who had thought Rosa was haughty at her wedding, warmed to her in her fallen state and included her in their gossip as they beat the soapy clothing and sheets on the smooth creek boulders and stretched them on the sunny bank to bleach. Rosa acted humble but secretly held her thought that Alejandro would come and take her away. Marilena's husband came frequently and shared a meal with her, but didn't take her away. Gomersinda's man—they had never married—was driven away and the door locked against him by Merceditas. There were two older girls who helped watch the infants that belonged to Marilena, and a boy who went to school.

Alejandro had told her his father was in the States sending back money. Gomersinda told her he was in jail. Merceditas never mentioned him.

Rosa noted that Merceditas rose at six every morning and went alone to Mass, so she began to rouse herself at this hour, too, to wash her face at the pump and put on a fresh blouse and accompany her mother-in-law down the dusty path that followed the highway, to a stairway leaning up to the Capilla de los Descalzos. She went to thank the Virgin, whose visitation seemed to fade in this sunny place, until she could scarcely feel it, as little by little her gratitude began to be replaced by a petition ... that Alejandro should come to her.

Some of the rich ladies from the vacation houses farther up the hill attended the chapel, as it was in their parish, and Rosa got up the courage to ask one of them if she needed a washerwoman. Eventually, this lady and another were accompanied by their maids carrying laundry baskets of sheets and towels, which Rosa returned a day later, washed and ironed. The money she earned she kept under a loose tile in a corner of the patio, so that she could offer it to Alejandro when he came.

So, a second time her prayers were answered, and the following month the man she had fled did come to her. Rosa, who had been washing at the creek, wasn't aware of his presence until he had been she didn't know how long in the little dark parlor with his mother, who was smoking her cigarette. The others were all napping, but Rosa no longer napped because she had so much washing. She stood unseen in the kitchen and overheard him complain of her, Rosa, in injured tones: She stole from me to come here ...

There was no answer from Merceditas, just as she had had no answer to Rosa's complaint a month ago. Did you hear what I said? Alejandro said.

I'm resting, said his mother. Tell me some other time.

Rosa went out to unearth the money, but then put it back, thinking she would wait for the best time. He came to her as she was rinsing out the bedclothes and hanging them over the bushes to dry. He had Mondo on his shoulders.

You come back, he said. He was sober.

She was coy.

I am doing the washing of two rich ladies. I pay you back all the money I took.

Okay. That's good. He went to play in the water with Mondo.

The result of this conversation was that he stayed a week without saying anything to her about going back, as if he had come for a long vacation, or worse to take up semipermanent residence, like Gomersinda's husband, Paco. Days, he went fishing with Paco. Sometimes he ate with them, sometimes not.

Nights he came to her in her hammock. My woman, he said, pulling up her slip and rubbing her belly and sucking her breasts until she became so wet she thought maybe her water had broken. He smelled of rum but he was gentle. Oh, she loved him.

But if he gave no thought to the mountain—to the hens, the cornfield, the tomatoes, the half-finished shed—she did. Who is feeding the hens? she asked him.

Your uncle, he said mildly, with no hint of the old suspicion that this was a man she slept with.

A week or more she waited to hear what he planned. She was becoming heavy. It was harder and harder to wash for the family and for the two rich ladies. She gave one of them to Marilena. If the daughters-in-law had had any gumption they would have found these jobs for themselves.

She was becoming heavy. She needed a home to prepare for this baby. She longed for her bed, her back was aching.

She could see that Alejandro was happy here. She had made a mistake, maybe, urging him up the mountain. The mountain made him worried and bitter.

What about the corn? she said one day when they were both playing with Mondo in the water. They had planted enough for themselves and some also to sell in the market. He threw Mondo up in the air, not answering her.

But later he said, I guess we should go up.

I need my bed, she said. I cannot push out a baby in that hammock. She made the comment lightly, with a smile to match his good humor.

Ah, *mujer. Mujeres!* He made a joke of her at the lunch table. What kind of woman can't have a baby in a hammock?

She sensed this was a good day to show him her money. She brought it out after lunch and gave it to him. For the pig, she said. Alejandro had consented to a pig as being less work than a cow, and Rosa had plans for piglets.

We must get the corn in, she said to him seriously.

So it was a little like returning from a honeymoon, getting back on the wide-bodied bus that left at midnight to arrive on the mountain before dawn. Merceditas saw them off with a face that concealed any doubts she might have had. And neither of them, neither Rosa nor Alejandro, had gotten from her what they had wanted.

As they rode along the darkened littoral, Rosa felt that she had almost been restored to her bridal good looks. The tiredness had lifted. She was swollen like a ripe fruit, sated with Alejandro's lovemaking. Their bundles contained some little clothing she had sewed for the new child, and she was wearing a new pleated blouse Merceditas had helped her make.

The bus strained up onto the mountain road, only the little pit where her molar had been reminded her of that other desperate nighttime ride. She put this out of her mind and anticipated what she would find at her home, picturing the row of maturing coffee bushes under the guava trees, the fat ears of corn, the expert framing of the pig stable. Maybe it was finished by now and she could go about bargaining for a pregnant sow. In the little time Alejandro was with his mother, he had finished an outdoor shower stall, whistling and humming all the while.

She must keep up her good humor too, she told herself. When it was cold and she just wanted to wrap herself up in blankets and sleep, she would instead light the stove and make cocoa and offer some to Alejandro and they would sit at the big table he had built and have conversations the way they did on the banks of the little creek while they played with Mondo. If the mountain was sometimes gloomy, she could not be. It had been her fault all along.

Rosa doesn't remember exactly when the life went out of Alejandro and into her.

They arrived on the mountain before dawn. The little house was muffled in a cloud as usual at this hour. She put the sleeping Mondo in his crib and firmly ignored the disorder and filth in all the rooms. There would be time for that. Then she collected the few wood scraps she could find and lit the stove. She had brought some powdered milk and cocoa and rolls from down below, fearing there would be no food. Wheat rolls were a treat in those days. She set them out along with two pretty cups that Merceditas had given her. Come, sit, she said to her husband and smiled at him.

The coming baby was leaping inside her and giving her a backache when she got up later to straighten and sweep the house. She brought in a basketful of tomatoes and squash and was started on the corn when Alejandro got up.

Where is the boy with the milk? Why is there no firewood? she wanted to say but didn't.

Her uncle came by to feed the chickens and was surprised to see her there. Alejandro ignored him and went for the milk.

I don't know how he lived all the time you were gone, her uncle said. Once he killed a chicken, the rest of the time he lived on rum.

It will be better, she said. Don't come anymore. She was patient; she smiled. I told my uncle not to come anymore. This child is yours, she whispered to him in bed. I swear it. He didn't answer.

I swear it by the Virgin. You were very silly to think such a thought, she teased. She was happy that day; they had sold the corn, and Alejandro was back to work on the pig house.

But he didn't answer. While Rosa became chatty, he became silent. Instead of coming to bed when she fell exhausted and slept almost immediately, he sat at the table in the kitchen far into the night. If she woke much later, still he wasn't in bed. Then he would sleep until late in the morning.

The shed was not quite finished but she allowed herself to pick out a half-grown female from a litter in the marketplace and reserve it for herself. She picked one with a black spot on its back and a tightly curled tail. Alejandro had left off keeping an account of the hens' laying while she was gone, so she updated the notebook and cooked the poorest layers one by one on Saturdays, replacing them with chicks from her aunt's roosting hens. She was careful to only go to her aunt after church on Sunday. A time when he expected her to be gone.

She didn't say much to her sisters or her aunt about her long absence. Especially to her sisters, as they had always been jealous of her and Alejandro. One, Rosalia, had actually moved to the capital to cure herself of a crush on him. Her aunt, who allowed herself on Sundays to fill the day with long gossips over cups of cocoa, expected more details, and Rosa let down her defenses once or twice, and didn't deny that Alejandro had hit her. He will hit you again, and harder, said her aunt.

No, he won't. I have changed. I make myself pretty and smile and cook nice things for him.

The trouble was that he had no appetite. Always, the meal was ready at the wrong time. Too late, and he was into his bottle. Too early, and he wasn't ready. Or, at odd times when nothing was prepared, he came foraging in the pantry and ate up all the sweets for an entire week.

She confessed to Father Clodomiro that she had trouble being a good wife.

Do you cook three times a day? he asked.

Yes.

Do you look after your children?

Oh, yes!

Do you allow him your bed?

Yes, yes!

Search in your heart then. There must be some impediment.

Rosa searched her heart and hid the misery this caused her.

Her aunt resembled Merceditas in the little pleasures she allowed herself. On Sundays she made a savory chicken stew that filled the house with its aroma. She always served herself last and sat longer than the young people, Rosa's brothers and sisters, who rushed away from the table, while one of them brought her an *infusion* of one of the herbs in her garden: manzanilla, or limoncillo. This treat her aunt drank slowly while she picked the meat off the back of the chicken with her fingers. She liked to have Mondo sit in her lap and pat his little hands together and slip him bits of the tender meat she found in the bony pockets of a chicken back. She had two other little nieces who visited, but liked to point out to Rosa all the ways in which Mondo surpassed them in sturdiness and cleverness.

And sometimes Rosa allowed these moments with her aunt to seduce her into staying away really longer than a good wife would. And then came the day she had to hurry home because she had a cardboard box full of hatchlings from her aunt's henhouse to settle in their new home; and, hating to deny her aunt the pleasure of Mondo, had left him there in her lap, planning to come back in the evening.

Where is the boy? Alejandro demanded above the clamor of the hens.

I left him there a couple hours, while I brought these chicks.

He didn't answer.

Listen, Rosa said, hoping to forestall whatever was unsaid behind his menacing face, when I ran away from you I ran to *your* mama, doesn't that tell you something?

She felt a cramp in her belly.

I took both of your children to your mother to be safe! she shouted. Then she had to go and lay down.

It was a month early for this baby. She felt she must be careful; but she must get the boy. When she got up, Alejandro was gone from the house. She started out down the path to her aunt's and met him coming along the opposite way with Mondo on his shoulders.

She turned back to the house and went to light the stove. She hoped Alejandro had been civil with her aunt. None of this was *her* fault.

He stood in the doorway. We'll eat in a few minutes. I hope my aunt didn't feed you already, she said pleasantly. The cramp had almost gone away, though she was still moving about carefully.

Did you think I was going to be like your daddy and give my children to her? he said.

What are you saying?

You hear me.

He give us to her because my mother die. It's not the same thing. How can you say such a ...

A hard cramp pierced her and took away her breath.

She had cleared the table of his rum bottle. Now he was looking for it.

She found it for him. Panic was coming over her. If this baby was wanting to be born, the midwife must be fetched. Would he even help her?

She sat down. Mondo crawled into her lap, Alejandro pulled him away.

You leave my house, he shouted, and swigged from the bottle.

Absurdly she thought of the new chicks, of the pig that was spoken for. Suddenly she felt so sorry for herself she began to weep.

Stop crying. I give you something to cry about.

She had her eyes closed, so she didn't see the blow coming.

She must have passed out. The black came before her face; then, when she became conscious, the pain gave her something real to cry about, as he had promised, wiped away thoughts of chicks, of pigs ... She held her jaw and tried to run to the bedroom. He blocked her way.

She ran outside and sat on the stoop. She heard him bar the door. She must run again to his mother, was her first thought. But another cramp put that out of her mind. The pain in her jaw became bearable only if she held it in a certain way with her hand. She could hear Mondo crying inside, and that cleared up her brain finally and told her she must get help.

Up the hill lived the Salazars. The people with the cow. The boy, Hugo, who delivered the milk, had a cart and mule. She started up the path he had worn with his morning rounds, holding her face together and stopping to double over when the cramp came. She wanted to moan, but that hurt too much.

Partway up she knew she wouldn't make it. The black came before her face again and she cried out to the Virgin.

She came to in the cart laying on a pile of burlap bags. One of Hugo's brothers was driving. He had taken her to the *abasto* down the road, where a call was put through from the only telephone in the district. She remembers passing out again as she was transferred to one of the *rurales* ambulances; and that her water broke as she was being carried into the little clinic in Los Gordos.

All the time she kept crying out that they must save Mondo, but no one understood her, as her jaw had been taped shut, trapping the words inside her mouth. Finally she was given pencil and paper and was able to write her message, but by then Alejandro had taken Mondo to his mother. He was two years old when she got him back, only because Alejandro was in the clinic having his leg taken off and her uncle was able to go and snatch him from among the cousins playing by the creek.

When Rosa thinks about sin now, it is this experience that makes her question Father Clodomiro's suggestion to think hard about why she wasn't being a good wife. Sin is when you get something you want too much, Rosa believes now. She wanted Alejandro too much, and her two babies were in danger that day she ran up the hill holding her face together, and the darkness...

She might never have seen Mondo again. He might have wandered away looking for her while his father lay unconscious. And Eva might have been born on that chilly mountainside and died with no one to help.

She doesn't speak about sin with priests anymore. Only with the Virgin, who understands women.

Is Wolfie a sin? She does want him too much. But then she thinks: who is harmed?

If God formed us to want too much, how can we not sin? But Wolfie doesn't feel like a sin.

Is she being punished by being kept away from him? Is Wolfie being punished by falling into the hands of the cruel Irishwoman?

These are questions she asks the Virgin. And she gets little bits of answers sometimes when she is walking out to Piety Corner.

She must talk to him if they are ever together again. They cannot just be two bodies touching. This is something the Virgin is telling her.

Her love must be strong enough to endure this waiting. It is like the time she lived at her aunt with the two children and had to keep going in spite of her sadness until she learned to do without Alejandro. To learn of his motorcycle accident when he lost his leg and not go to him. To be a woman alone and to come to Lawrence, Massachusetts. A testing time.

But Wolfie? The Virgin hasn't explained Wolfie's suffering to her yet. Maybe Wolfie himself needs to find a way to speak, to complain to the agency. To be bold like that day his penis stood up. Oh, Wolfie.

The Virgin, Rosa thinks, the Virgin saved her that time. She will save me again maybe. She wishes she had told Esmeralda at least the part about the Virgin coming to her.

But the other thing Rosa could never tell Esmeralda, or her catechism students in the past, is a shocking thought she has about the Virgin ...

Maybe she wasn't a virgin at all.

Maybe a brother or an uncle was the father of Jesus. This thought doesn't bother Rosa very much in regard to her own love of Her. To Rosa she is still a virgin, still to be worshipped; but she knows that for most people, this thought would bring down their whole Catholic faith.

Part of this conjecture has to do with her youngest sister, Patricia. While the other three of them were verbally agile and loud, and made good grades in school, Patricia barely talked until she was four, and after that spoke in such a soft voice that they all barely listened to her. Her teachers in the school were always calling their uncle in over her failure to learn to read and write, and he scolded her so much that the little girl asked if she could stay home and help in the house. Their aunt didn't approve of this, and even Rosa, who had tried to help her read, felt bad about it. But finally they all gave in and forgot about the matter.

When they went back to their father, the arrangement continued, and no one even thought about it anymore. The three of them continued being good readers and multipliers and dividers, and falling into fits of giggles over almost everything that happened in spite of the trials of living with their father, and now Patricia helped both her father and her aunt and often spent overnights with her aunt and uncle, because she loved her aunt and was afraid of their father. And no one much spoke to her or noticed her.

Then one after another they all got their bleeding, but not Patricia; and when they found out why, everybody noticed her.

She had a belly that just kept growing. Their aunt suggested that perhaps her periods were getting stuck inside her. But that theory couldn't hold up for long, and when she had just turned thirteen she had this baby on the floor of their latrine. She got up after from the packed mud floor, cleaned herself, and brought the child to show her sisters.

He was very skinny always; they tried in vain to fatten him; but the little boy lived, and the little girl lovingly took care of him. Their father was pleased; he thought his wife's death deprived him of all the sons he should have had. There were no more theories of any kind about why her belly kept growing.

Rosa alternately blamed her father and her uncle, and never resolved this question, though it had been her uncle who had tried to make advances to her and been scared away by her loud protests; probably all three of them were too noisy for him, but not Patricia.

When Rosa tries to imagine how Patricia felt about all of this, she never gets quite to the end of her thoughts, but the matter comes into her head a lot. They barely noticed it, but all of Patricia's education came from catechism classes, which unlike school she went to happily. She was a good memorizer, so good that once Rosa came upon her resting in a rocking chair reciting to herself a long, really long, part of the Bible almost as if she was reading it. It went on and on, without a stumble ... This was an uncanny thing that Rosa never forgot.

Maybe the little girl used these stories to make sense of her mute life. Maybe as the child grew in her and brought the pains on her on the floor of that latrine, they were all she had to make sense of what was happening to her.

Did she know, even, Rosa thinks now, what was sex?

The other three of them had hold of parts of the story. These they found gruesome and hilarious. They were mostly what they giggled about. "Oh, I need to go to the latrine. Maybe it's a baby coming out!" Patricia was never part of this silliness. Every one of their school friends knew some part of the sex story, depending on how much their parents let out, so they didn't really miss out by not having their own mother. And they were good readers. They found much more interesting things to read than the Bible stories that Patricia knew by heart. There were the *fotonovelas* for sale at the *abasto*, with their photos and speech balloons based on the romantic soap operas on the radio. These satisfied them for a while but were rather formal and couldn't really show you much sex beyond kissing in a photograph. They found out more after moving on to the *centavo* paperbacks, whose pages fell out by the time they were passed to the third or fourth reader; and even a sex manual someone found in her house. And of course the boys told them things.

Rape-proof, we were, Rosa thinks, smart alecky, noisy, and rape proof.

But what could Patricia have thought about her uncle's huffing and puffing on top of her? Maybe she wasn't even awake. She seemed as innocent after the birth as before, as much a virgin as before. Was she really still a virgin? By all the standards Rosa knew, she was more innocent than her three noisy sisters.

Is this what happened to Mary? Rosa tries to follow this thought on a warm day as she picks dead things out of her garden, thinking of spring creeping up.

They didn't think Jesus could read. Could his Mother?

Like Patricia, she must have had the stories by heart. In her heart. Or in her belly, her womb…

Babies came because you asked God for them, like Hannah asked for Samuel.

Rosa forgets the name the boy was given; she went to live with Alejandro soon after and found out all she ever needed to know about sex. It was an odd name, the middle one… The first name, which he went by, might have been Francisco like their father; but no one knew where the second name came from and tried to talk Patricia out of it. But she could be stubborn.

He's my baby, she said, and seemed to gain some ascendancy over them from then on.

But after Rosa learned the final secrets about sex, she tried to imagine how sex had come, all unexplained, to Patricia.

Her uncle, certainly, had access to them all. The youngest, Tito, Patricia, Lucha, and Rosa, all slept at one time in the big bed with their aunt and uncle. But she can't imagine any huffing and pumping above any one of them with their aunt in the bed too.

And how did her aunt and uncle ever do it together, with all these children in their bed?

This is the first time Rosa's ever had this thought, and she pursues it after she goes in and washes her muddy hands and sets the rice to boil.

Her uncle must have developed a way of doing it, even with his wife, in a way Rosa's never experienced. When Rosa dreams of Wolfie coming to her in a bed, she imagines it as it must have been with Patricia, awakening out of sleep at a gentle insinuation, teasing her into a receptive state, requiring of her not the slightest movement or wakefulness. Until it comes, the ravishing...

But with Patricia, the uncle's sin, as soon as it is delivered into her womb, is purified by Patricia's innocence. Of this, Rosa is sure. Of all the sisters, she is the pure one, still.

Unlike the four rapid readers shrieking over the revelations in the yellowed, falling-out pages of the *centavo novellas* from the bodega, she couldn't, wouldn't, read, knew only the stories she had memorized in catechism.

Rosa is all in a sweat and turns on the kitchen fan before lowering the flame under the rice. An eggplant needs to be used up, and she cuts it into the rice, along with some cilantro and a zucchini.

Rosa tries to think what were the stories in Patricia's head: Sarah and Abraham, Isaac and Rachel, Hannah and Samuel, Mary and Joseph; except for Mary, women longing for children ... and when a child arrives, it is a special child ...

What was the boy's name? Did he live and grow up to help their father? He would be one year older than Mondo ...

It was such an odd name. They repeated it over, trying to make sense of it.

Rosa is absently fixing herself a bowl of farina and a cup of coffee, and sees she has filled her coffee cup with farina.

Madre! She shakes herself, pours out the mess. She has become again the dreamy housekeeper who lived with her father and moped around while Patricia did all the work.

She served them all and never complained. And they thought it was her job, since she wouldn't go to school.

Francisco Jesús ... These were both names from the family: Francisco, the father, and Jesús, their uncle, and the third name ...

Francisco Jesús Samuel Flores! There it was.

Two family names, and then that strange one they had tried to make her give up.

Hannah.

Hannah who shrieked for a child in the temple. The priests thought she was drunk.

He would be a little older than Mondo.

But there was no sin in Patricia, Rosa knows. Just like there was no sin in Jesus when they crucified Him.

... took away the sin of the world. She never understood before what that meant. Patricia took away the sin of their uncle.

He would be a little older than Mondo, she thinks. She's not sure ...

And there is no one left in Xoyatla to write to…

III.
Eulalie

Eulalie Arsenault is truly dying now. Alcide has left off his roaming ways and wants to sit by her side and gloomily survey her wracked body as they turn her every hour and dress her cratered chest wall, and lay her arm, swollen like a gaseous bladder, on a pillow. Only her legs remain alive, shapely and muscular; and Alcide rests his head on the bed, clinging to an ankle.

The night she told me about the lump we make love all night on the floor, he tells Rosa. On the floor?

I fall down when she was out. She come home and can't lift me, so we put pillows and sleep there. Her mother had the lump too. But Lalie don't let them cut her.

At the end they had to cut her, to remove some of the rot. But that cutting had only made the arm swell up to an unimaginable size, its gases seeping out onto the pillow and smelling of horror. Now I've seen cancer, Rosa thinks, wondering why it can't be over quicker. Eulalie seems to be asleep most of the time and Rosa tries not to wake her when she comes in to turn her over. Nurses have told them not to try to make her eat, that it's more comfortable to die of starvation than of cancer. She has a drip of morphine now, and hopefully she's dreaming of the Emerald Isle Quadrille and of kitchen rackets and of her newest dance dress she's confecting on the old treadle sewing machine that still sits at the foot of her bed. Poor Eulalie.

There is a daughter who comes from New York and stays a week and then goes home. She will return when needed, she tells Priscilla. The unfortunate daughter looks like Alcide, has none of Eulalie's beauty, and has never married.

There isn't time to call the daughter as it turns out. Rosa finds her dead on Wednesday midmorning and calls Priscilla and the Hospice. A nurse comes and takes out the IV and pours what Priscilla says must be a couple thousand dollars of morphine down the sink. The three of them wash the body while Alcide watches. They feel giddy and happy for Eulalie, and oddly alive. When they are finished they take Alcide down to the Red Rooster for lunch. He cheers up over an omelet.

I give her a good life.

Yes, you did, Alcide.

We both work at the mill before we marry. I have my army pay and I learn electricity at the Arsenal. Then I work at the Arsenal for good salary and Eulalie work at the Buckle. When we marry I don't let her work. She stays home with the little girl and sews her dresses and every Saturday we go to dances at Nuttings. Eulalie is always the best-looking girl there.

I bet she was, says the nurse, who has a kind face and is a good friend of Priscilla's.

Before we marry she would never step one step in there, says Alcide. After, with me, she can go anywhere. Still, she is strict with herself. She will go to Nuttings, but there are still places she won't go. Anyplace there might be Bolsheviks. She get that from the teachers at the Adult Education. My Eulalie. Those teachers make my life hell before I marry. I am going so crazy, I need to go to the bad girls, and then Eulalie find out and never forgive me.

You'll miss her, says the nurse. And there is such a look of desolation on Alcide's face that Rosa thinks that now he can flee away from Eulalie whenever he wants, he probably never will again.

IV.
Two Mediterranean Ladies

Rosa finishes embroidering the basket of flowers and is given a basket of kittens to stitch. Kittens are more difficult than flowers and she must pull out some mistaken stitches and redo them with Gina's help. She's never known a woman who did these handcrafts. In Xoyatla they wove in big, bold stripes, blankets for the beds and ponchos for the *invierno*. If not for this strange assignment, she never would have taken the time to do such tiny, useless things. Still, the results are pretty, and she has sewn the flower basket into a pretty pillow to give to Eva for Christmas. Maybe she will give the kittens to Esmeralda. She is still nervous with Gina, and prefers to work at home where she can forgive herself little errors that no one but Gina will see.

Late afternoons are the most grateful time with Gina. Soon she can leave and there is just one more sitting down to the deep chocolate bars and the strong, milky coffee. Rosa relaxes and offers up some of the words they share: *rico, bien caliente, sabroso*... Other than *filia*, daughter, she has learned to say none of Gina's words—though she understands many of them—and Gina has learned none of Rosa's words; so that their conversations have not progressed much beyond the first day's revelations. If she were really Spanish, Rosa is sure, she would by now be chatting away easily. Also Gina firmly misunderstands any attempt to convey her wish to leap up and wash up as if there were no equivalent in Italian to the words *lavar*, *barrer*, etc.

In an effort to make the hours go a little more quickly, Rosa has brought a little Xeroxed map of the Mediterranean provided by Esmeralda, and Gina has eagerly pointed out Turin, where she is from, and Rome, where her husband sang opera, and the Amalfi coast, where they went to swim, Rosa thinks she understands. Also a town called Montanesa, where husband and *filio* were buried.

Also they look at Spain, where Gina once visited Toledo and Madrid. Rosa is not familiar with these places, but is able to tell Gina that her *esposo*'s grandfather came from Galicia, and to point to this place on the map. Laureano, of course, is not her *esposo*; but for the sake of simplicity and available words she is not going to be fussy.

That week the weather turns nasty, and they find the nanny shivering behind the garage nursing two tiny spotted kids. Rosa moves them into the back room where the washing machine is and lines the floor with newspapers. When she comes home afternoons she brings one of the kids into the kitchen and holds him in her lap while she has a cup of chamomile tea to calm her stomach after Gina's strong coffee and all the little delicacies. Soon they are following her all over the house on their tender little hooves, and even Laureano is smitten. He is spending more time in the house with her lately, probably because of the weather, but he complains he gets out of breath more easily than he used to.

Well, you're an old man, says Rosa.

Not old. My father wasn't old till he was seventy-eight.

Well, he wasn't walking around on roofs.

He built a house when he was my age.

What age was that?

Sixty-four.

You are seventy.

What makes you say that?

It's on your drivers' license.

I lied when I was thirteen, so I could drive.

You can't do that.

Where I was back then you could.

He lies, she thinks; but by now he probably even believes this story himself. She's seen his age on his Social Security documents as well. He is seventy.

The little goat she has named Blanca is nibbling on her shoe. She wishes Gina could see her goats. Maybe her daughter will bring her.

V.
Christmas

Eva is coming and Mondo has a three-day pass. Friday the *matadero* comes for the billy, takes him behind the garage, and does his business. The meat, minus one haunch—payment for the *matadero*—is stored in the basement entrance until Saturday, when Laureano starts the fire in the brick grill he built beside the garage. Meanwhile Rosa boils a foreleg with onions and cilantro. Lidia, Laureano's daughter, calls to say she's coming with her baby next afternoon. As always, the last minute. And where did this baby come from?

She'll probably bring the baby's father. And Laureano's twin sons, Sami and Vicente, will arrive Christmas Day. She doesn't like the thought of Mondo and Sami getting together, but what can she do...

Let Eva give them fair warning about spoiling the day. She'll make them eat something, and not start drinking until evening. Vicente goes to those AA meetings and has started technical college. She knows Mrs. Rose at the Sunshine Club goes to that AA and has not had a drink in fifteen years.

Alejandro was a drinker. It's who I am, he used to say. I drink. Mondo got it from him.

She has to work Monday, so she makes the tamale *masa* Sunday night from a hand of *verdes* that's been hanging in the laundry room for a week, then adds the pork and the little peas from a can and the onions and carrots. They are all neatly wrapped in corn husks and set out in the back porch when she leaves at seven to give Clifford's bath.

She finds him naked at the dining room table, writing figures in one of his notebooks. Happy Christmas, she says.

Eh ... what's that?

Christmas. She feels flush with happiness.

The baby Jesus is coming, she says, recalling her aunt scolding them to get ready to come in from playing with *estrellitas* and to comb their hair and wash their faces and pray the last prayer of the *novena* in front of the crèche she always made on a makeshift table on the veranda. It had little lakes made from broken mirrors and real moss and a sandy desert where the Magi approached. Mary and Joseph stood in the stable before an empty manger; for the Niño could not come until midnight, until all the faces were clean and the hair combed and all the nine prayers said.

Because of her aunt, Rosa always did all these things with her own children while they were young. She could still do them, she thinks. Laureano will laugh, but he has his ceremonies with the cook fire. And there will be one child this year, innocent of its father and mother's sins, like her own two used to be ... And Eva is coming with her young man, so maybe there will be another child next year.

We have to get ready for the Baby Jesus, she tells Clifford while she runs his bath.

He clears his throat and rubs his belly, then pees his feeble stream and steps into the tub.

Were you ever married, Clifford? she asks.

Once, he grunts.

Did you have children?

No children, he says.

How sad. She wonders if Mrs. Rose's children have come. Mrs. Rose had four children. One is dead, and she only knows where one of the others is. And Wolfie's two sons...

There isn't much time, but when she gets home Rosa is able to find the plaster crèche set under the spare bed in the attic. She just has it finished, including a little desert and a lake of silver foil, when Lidia arrives, alone, with a six-month-old son. He claps and crows over the scene and is given a king to hold.

I'm going to be married, Lidia tells her. To a big red-haired gringo, thinks Rosa, judging by the strapping baby.

Not to the baby's father, Lidia tells her. This one is a good man. He works all the time. He's working today. I'm going to settle down, she says, no more booze.

Rosa hopes it's so. Why do we have these alcoholic children, she wonders, why does the Virgin allow it?

Me purifica. He purifies me, her aunt used to say when her uncle went out drinking three days straight. The Virgin must have her reasons, Rosa thinks. She squeezes Lidia to her and leads her to the kitchen to help make the yellow rice and peas.

All day, she imagines The Virgin watching her. Eva comes. So beautiful. Eva's beauty is foreign to Rosa. She is tall, coffee-colored, slender. One of Alejandro's people from the languid coast. She has her father's gifts, but Rosa's energy.

There is a four-star general now in the government who is Eva's color. The Army made him. Eva sensed since high school that the Army could make her, and she was right. With her is a lanky boy, her color, in uniform. His name is Deroy, and he is only a corporal, but the Army will make him too, she thinks. His family is from Cleveland. They are leaving tomorrow night to go to his family. Rosa is thrilled with him; and when Laureano comes in with a bottle of rum, he and Lidia both say no.

Thank you, thank you, she tells the Virgin.

Sometimes it is the Virgin watching Rosa being happy, sometimes it is Wolfie, and other times it is the agency. The agency must think something bad about Rosa, or they wouldn't have taken Wolfie away from her.

Wolfie does have a holiday visitor. One of his sons. He is talking to Rebecca when Rosa brings Winnie in. Like his father, he has a plume of hair that falls over his forehead, but, while Wolfie's hair is still black black, the son's hair is half gray. It must be the son who bought the keyboard, for he next takes Rebecca over to demonstrate some wonder of this apparatus. Priscilla is looking on too. She wishes she could look, but doesn't want to offend the agency, who might be spying. Even so, she hopes they do spy so that they might one day get on to Mrs. Fahey. After lunch she gets a minute with Priscilla.

You talk to Wolfie's son? Can you tell me what he say?

He wants Rebecca to teach him, or find him a teacher. I said I would help.

What you teach him?

Well, to type, basically. You never find a man who's learned to type. If he can learn to type faster, the machine will talk for him. He's slow. He can say some things, but slow. The machine can talk? says Rosa.

Well, it will when he learns to type. Right now you can read on the screen what he says. But he doesn't say much. He needs to *want* to talk, Rebecca thinks.

He doesn't want to?

They think he's depressed.

Ah, Wolfie. He was never depressed with her, Rosa thinks.

But you will help him.

I can try. If he will try.

VI.
Lidia

She is busy with Lidia's baby the whole next week. Lidia needs to look for a job. Laureano says she can stay with the baby in the attic bedroom if she will find a job and keep it. So here they are again with diapers and bottles and soggy sheets. Little Beatrice downstairs says she will watch the baby together with her own; but Rosa isn't very sure of her so keeps about the place watching. The Guatemalan baby has been swaddled since birth, while Lidia's baby is climbing out of strollers and cribs, and cruising around the room holding onto walls. She doesn't think Beatrice is prepared for this kind of baby, who reminds Rosa of Mondo at this age. Finally, she turns to little Esmeralda for help; and, by the end of the week, little Michael is cruising around behind the counters of the Mexican store and sucking on pieces of sugarcane given him by Esmeralda and her sisters, Lidia has a job at the lumberyard, and Laureano is boasting about *ese gallo bravo*, who is his grandson, diapering him in front of the whole world and showing off his sturdy legs and stiff little manhood.

The new, serious Lidia brings the hardworking Max to live in the attic room with her. He is so hardworking that he is hardly ever seen, going off on his bicycle at 7:30 in the morning and not returning until everyone is asleep. In one of his jobs he is a short-order cook; in the other two he does "sheerock" like all the other Mexicans. Lidia works three to eleven, and in the mornings she helps in the house, setting the washing machine going at seven and putting on the coffee and the rice to cook. Most days she sets a chicken to boil or a piece of rump meat, so that there's a soup for lunch and a start on dinner. Rosa is grateful and goes to work with an easier mind than she has in years. And every evening Lidia leaves little Michael at the Mexican store and goes to one of those AA meetings in the church hall basement of the Italian church.

At the Sunshine Club Rosa asks Mrs. Rose about these meetings. What people do there?

Well, you have to tell your story. Every dreadful detail. Yes. And tell people you're sorry.

And that makes people better?

It's a miracle of sorts. And you have to believe in God. Any sort of god will do.

And that's all?

Well, and you can't ever lie. And you have to try to help the others. I think that's it.

What about the saints? Rosa asks, then feels abashed; but Mrs. Rose says, well, they could probably help. Then she tells Rosa about a man she knew who believed in a light bulb, and another who believed in trees, and they both got sober.

Rosa looks so crushed by this that Mrs. Rose says kindly that she thinks the saints are much more likely to produce a better kind of sobriety, and that if she knew more about them she would probably call on them, that in fact she often prayed to her mother-in-law, who she considered a kind of saint. She asks Rosa to tell her something about one of the saints, because her church, the big white Congregational church downtown, never brings them up.

Rosa knows several saints, from her aunt. Her favorite is Teresita. She tells Mrs. Rose about the time the child Teresita and one of her kin ran away. They wanted to go to Africa and become martyrs. Their uncle saw them on the road and brought them home. Rosa loves this story. It was Teresita who helped her to pack herself up and come here.

Here, Mrs. Rose asks her if she could bring her another cup of tea; so Rosa goes and gets it, and by the time she returns she has thought of Saint Rita.

Saint Rita had a husband and a son who drank too much, she tells Mrs. Rose.

You don't say.

One day she wished them dead.

A saint…?

Well, she wasn't a saint yet. Some saints don't even know they going to become saints.

That's very interesting. I don't know why Protestants shy away from the saints. Fear of popery, I suspect.

Well, and then right away they did die.

Who?

The husband and the son.

Ah, lucky for her. We alcoholics are no fun to live with.

But she feel terrible.

Oh.

She thought she kill them.

Ah. Mrs. Rose, who has a son who drinks and sponges off her and frequently makes her unhappy because she loves him so much, can understand this perfectly.

She go to a convent and ask them to let her in. She is being punished by a bad smell. No one can go near her, so they put her in a cell all by herself.

How dreadful.

And that's how was her life. Bad smell, and she pray for everyone and do good works.

Rosa feels she hasn't told this story very well, but Mrs. Rose seems moved. She thinks of Alejandro and Mondo and her uncle. *Me purifica*, her aunt used to say of her husband. He purifies me. Do Alejandro and Mondo purify her, Rosa? Does Mrs. Rose's son purify her? Why do she need purifying and not Mondo?

VII.
Another Death

Were these questions preparing her? Was Eulalie's death preparing her?

They must have been, for on the following Tuesday, one of her days with Gina, she comes home from filling in another basket of kittens in three shades of gray yarn and being served little dainty cakes and fish pies to find Lidia and Esmeralda looking all over the house for Laureano.

They haven't seen him since eleven o'clock. Rosa never pauses to help them search the house, but goes immediately to where she knows he will be: somewhere on the little shortcut he takes by the river, which brings him up behind the Mexican store.

The River Charles. All her life she lives by a river. The River Plata in Xoyatla. The River Merrimack in Lowell. The River Shawsheen in Billerica—not a very important river, but large enough to be that familiar moving presence behind the house. When Laureano wanted to move them here from Billerica, he showed her several houses. She chose this one because of the river, and Laureano came to love it too. He made a little pier of logs and tied up a rowboat he loved to sit in fishing for carp, which were actually people's pet goldfish released to grow long and fat. Along its shore which looked across to the old Bleachery, and where the *morenos* came to fish, he made a little path, a shortcut to the Mexican store, where he goes to buy cigarettes. Ladyslippers grow here, and skunk cabbage. This part of the river is wide and lazy, losing its current to seep into many little inlets.

She doesn't want to alarm herself. Probably he is arguing something with Don *Amable* at the store. Or, at the worst, had one of his little breathless spells and Esmeralda's mother or sisters are boiling him a little *infusion* of *manzanillo* to restore him before he starts back.

She will surely meet him on the path. To fortify this belief she walks her usual walk, noting a lovely grass with red stems and reddish plumes, picking the dry centers of last year's wild *margaritas* and putting them in her pocket to sow in her front garden, disapproving the pressed-down circles of grass with their strewn beer cans. The river by her side causes her to recall a dream she has of swimming in the river, starting just below the falls and floating past the Brandeis Castle—which was not right because that was above the falls, and also because she couldn't swim—then the Watch Factory and Mount Feake Cemetery, and, carried by the current, on to Watertown and Lewando's Laundry and the park and the little tunnels for bicycles, and Harvard University and Storrow Drive and on under the bridges to where the docks were and the big storage tanks for oil, and finally great ocean liners were passing her... What a crazy dream, and she'd had it more than once. Then she thinks of Priscilla telling her how during the years of poverty after her divorce, she told her children they were rich because the river was theirs. *My river*, she called it.

Because it's free, she told the children, then went on to tell them she owned the Green Line that took them to the docks, and a boat they took to an island she owned where you could camp free. Did they believe you? Rosa asked.

Two of them did. Well, they pretended to... Solie always wanted me to have money, like we did when I was married. Real stuff.

Oh, Priscilla is an odd girl. She never knew anyone like Priscilla. Except maybe Wolfie when he was himself... Thinking of Priscilla causes her to remember the strike, which is to start in two weeks. They are to get everyone to the Sunshine Club and leave two people to help Rebecca, then take to the streets with the signs they are to paint at Priscilla's apartment on Saturday. No one is to be on the clock. The Social Services—Rosa thinks here of Mondo's social workers—will step in here of course and take care of the invalids, they are not to worry about them. That will be hard to do, thinks Rosa, although she thinks pleasantly that at least Mrs. Fahey will not be able to be with Wolfie. Maybe he will have a nice social worker, an educated person, to bathe him...

She can't imagine Mrs. Fahey walking the streets with a sign on a pole. Probably she will cheat and stay home comfortably with her husband, who gives her everything she wants after all...

She steps out of a clearing where people have stored boats wrapped in blue vinyl and is already behind the Mexican store, which shocks her. She didn't meet Laureano, and she was sure she would.

Ah, Missus, Esmeralda's mother calls to her. He was here and he looked so pale, we made him sit down and gave him some coffee. We want him to stay and we call you, but he must go, he say. And he go. Maybe three hours ago.

Rosa knows then she must look more closely on the way back. Even though she once imagined one day she would find him fallen at the foot of the ladder he used to inspect the roof, rather than along this path where the *morenos* come to fish, she is not surprised. She imagines him stopping to smoke, sitting on one of the boulders lining the riverbank.

And, halfway back, hurrying now, here he is; legs still clinging to a large rock, and his head against a smaller, flattish stone behind him, at a cruel angle, halfway in the water, though he doesn't look drowned—surprised, rather—when she straightens him out and holds his head on her knee. She's able to pull him onto a little pebbly ledge, where she leaves him to go call for the ambulance.

It all passes like a scene organized by others, that she has very little part in, from that afternoon to his burial on Saturday. She tries to be as invisible as possible as Lidia and the twins and Mrs. Connor next door, who had been Yvonne's best friend, and Yvonne herself, his ex-wife, take over.

The Mass is taken by Father Sutherland, not Father Riley. Laureano managed to offend the gringo priest the few times he went to the five o'clock. Your sermon I find *estrambótico*, he said once to Father Riley. The priest said, Thank you very much, but must have later looked up the word; so there was a coolness even toward Rosa. He ought to use a dictionary more often, Laureano said.

Father Sutherland's sermon pleased Rosa. He hadn't known Laureano, but took some time to talk to Lidia before the Mass, and talked about him as father to three and Builder of Many Houses, who always spoke his mind—this last possibly a reference to Father Riley. To Rosa's mind, this summed up her Laureano, her man, as she was his woman. She never tried to change him, and now he was changeless.

The Spanish congregation for the next Mass was coming in by the time they had some coffee and coffee cake in the parish hall, so her friends Ermelinda and Elba Restrepo came up to hug her, as well as some Mexican ladies whose names escaped her. They evidently expected her to cry, but she was unable to. Then the gringo priest came up and wrung her hand and said in his unfortunate Spanish, I am very unfortunate, my darling Mrs. Flores.

I am a widow, thinks Rosa after it's all over, and immediately corrects herself. He never marry me, she thinks bitterly. So now I can't be even a widow. Still, everyone, except for Mrs. Connor next door, treats her as if she were, so for a week or so she acts like one: she moans and covers her face with her scarf in the Spanish Mass, and thinks of all the good times with Laureano and how life won't be the same without him. Even she is able to howl once or twice, the way the Mexicans do.

But in the end she is purified, like her aunt. Laureano has purified her, so she can leave off the widow business.

Of course there is no will, and Rosa prepares herself to turn the house over to Laureano's children, who have been tearing it apart in search of some directive. Almost a week after the funeral, however, a paper is found in his sock drawer under the little basin where he kept the lower dentures he seldom used.

TODO PARA EL GALLO BRAVO, he has scrawled, and signed with his name.

This is a complication. Rosa is asked by Mr. Zapata, the lawyer, what she thinks it means. He knows there was no marriage, yet he keeps including her in the investigation.

It means he has a seven-month-old grandson, she explains, recalling his pride in diapering the child. And the grandson hasn't had a chance yet to disappoint him like the sons and daughter, her instinct tells her.

This changes a great deal: it means that Lidia is custodian of the house and the money, and that the two sons have nothing to say.

It's a good thing that it's the new Lidia, thinks Rosa.

The first thing the new Lidia does is to put the hardworking Max in charge of the money. He negotiates a small loan to the twins with the assumption it won't be paid back. Then he calls Rosa up to the attic bedroom, which she finds surprisingly neat and clean in spite of three people living in it, and asks her to sit on the bed. He has a paper all prepared for her, neatly typed and signed by himself and Lidia.

She tries to read it, but her head is swimming; so he explains it.

We want you to stay.

Ah, now, I have no right.

We want you. Sr. Zapata has notarized this paper, you see.

She runs her finger over the little raised disc.

La queremos a Usted, he repeats. Max is from Ecuador, and uses the formal *usted.* She finds this unfamiliar and charming, so becomes even more shy of him. When she goes back downstairs, she sits in the kitchen awhile to think. They want her. She is needed to look after the Guatemalans, to contribute her small income if she wants. *If she wants*... If she doesn't want, she can just stay home and take care of things and watch her soap opera. Of course she won't do that. Doesn't he work three jobs?

A usted la queremos mucho, Max says. She hastens to thank St. Teresa and the Virgin, and St. Rita for good measure.

The house is like a heaven on earth. Little Michael walks now, at ten months. Like Mondo. He is so strong he turns the wheelbarrow over and drags it around. He butts heads with the goats. There is money now to pay Esmeralda's older sister, out of school, to care for him. And money to repair the porch and the bulkhead. Mondo is released now and living in a halfway house. He works on the house weekends, and they pay him. Like his father, he does careful work, making Max pay for the best materials instead of the cheap stuff the thrifty Max would choose. This house is an investment, he goes around saying, though he certainly has no legal stake in it, nor does she.

Though soon she finds otherwise. Lidia and Max are going to marry, and while they are at the paperwork, they discover that, since she and Laureano have been together twenty years, they are married under Common Law. The house is hers to claim while she lives; but of course she won't.

But she is a widow. She exploits this a little bit and takes to telling Mrs. Rose and Gina what a good man

Laureano had been and how she will miss him. Mrs. Rose takes this coldly, but not Gina, and one day a huge, satiny sympathy card comes from Gina Garofalo and *fil-ia*. It is the only one, and she sticks it in the frame of her vanity mirror with satisfaction.

In it is a little note saying that Gina would like to visit and see the little goat. May they come ...?

VIII.
A Visit

Rosa is thrown into a frenzy of straightening up. The goats are moved to the garage. Only on the coldest days does Rosa bring them in. Mondo, who is around now more than he is at the halfway house, is pestered into moving his derelict cars back behind the garage and the two broken washing machines into the storeroom in the basement. The plaster Virgin in the dining room is sponged off, as well as the leaves of the rubber tree, which has grown as high as the ceiling. Thanks to her aunt's teaching, kitchen and bathroom can stand any inspection. Only when all this is accomplished does Rosa set a date, the first Sunday in March, for Gina to come.

They arrive after ten o'clock mass in a long gray Mercedes Benz. Mondo, who still has not found a job, has been sent to the Mexican store for a *tres leches* cake baked specially for this occasion by Esmeralda's mother. While Rose waits decorously at the kitchen table, Mondo goes out to greet the two Italian ladies and to show them the backyard and the river view.

What a glorious property, the doctor daughter tells Rosa when they come in. *Bello, bello*, says Gina.

Yes, it is nice, says Rosa modestly. She has always known her yard and its view, if it had been on the other side of the river, would be a prime lot. The blacks and Latinos who live here only appreciate the fishing, but Rosa knows what a good value in land Laureano has invested in. One day the body shops and storefront Pentecostal churches would be cleared away, and the town's wealthy would want to put something pretty here.

Mondo has brought in Blanca and set her in Rosa's lap. It is a charming sight, and Gina can't stop exclaiming over it. Now I can't get up, she complains, but Mondo nicely brings the cake and a cake knife to the doctor and serves the coffee himself while the doctor cuts the cake and serves it on Rosa's best plates. The long gray Mercedes Benz has impressed him.

Bella, bella, la Bianca! Gina exclaims.

Now I'll have to get her a goat, says the doctor ruefully.

A goat should not be in the kitchen, Rosa scolds, and puts Blanca down on her little hooves, which have hardened up and now make a clatter on the tiles.

In the country, in Italy, goats come in the house, says the doctor. When I first brought my mother here and she saw all the big green yards where I live, she thought it was a farm. This she repeats to Gina in Italian. She didn't understand a suburb. If I just had a cow and some chickens, she could be happier there, she tells me. I don't know what to do, she is so unhappy. I thought she would love my pretty house . . .

But there is no one to talk to. The houses are far apart, and everyone is at work. And she wouldn't be able to talk to anyone anyhow. When we go to shop downtown at the supermarket on Main Street, she tells me she wants to live there over a store! She knows she can't talk to the people, but she wants them close around. I had forgotten that is the way in Italy: you live in the country or in the city; there is no in-between.

It is how it is in my country, says Rosa. We not suppose to have these goat. Before, my husband try to keep the cocks and the chickens and always there is trouble.

I had forgotten. I don't know what we would do without you. If you could give us another day, I would be so grateful. Rosa doesn't think she could sit still and do needlework another whole day.

Lidia comes down with Michael at this moment, and Gina, who had been crooning *bella, bella* over the little goat, throws up her hands in delight and goes to kiss the baby. The daughter looks at her sadly.

She has no child, thinks Rosa. There is no husband... She is an attractive woman, but not quite young. Probably she is forty...

There were only two of us, says the doctor. My brother and I. And neither of us had a child, though he was married; and now he is dead.

That is too bad, says Rosa. But maybe someday...

No, probably not. I give her what I can. I must have my life.

Rosa finds this very sad.

Perhaps you can bring the baby sometimes.

Hokay. Rosa likes this idea. It will relieve her of the tedium of the basket of kittens, and making conversations with the few words they can share.

IX.
Her Bad English

Everything is so beautiful around the new household, and there is so much more time for Rosa to simply sit in Laureano's recliner and think about her good fortune that, while Max and Mondo go about fixing the house, she can also think about fixing up herself, things like her bad English. No more Esmeralda coming around all the time, and she can't really just sit and talk to Mrs. Rose while she's supposed to be working.

Will the classes in the library take her back? Finally, she gets out of the recliner to go see.

The classes used to start at 6 p.m., so Rosa goes next day at this hour. The rooms are the same, but no familiar faces. A white-haired man is the new director, Mr. Fitzgerald. He gives her an application form to fill out and sits her down in an empty room to take a test. Afraid as always of being put in an advanced class, she fills in some answers she knows are wrong and answers all the "do" and "did" questions as best she can, but knows they aren't right. A half hour later, she is put in the beginner's class where she started out, with Miss Ann Marie, who looks about seventeen but is very brisk and has them stand up and do exercises while they repeat "Touch your knees," "Bend your arms," "Roll your shoulders." This is to wake up the people who work two jobs. Then she has the Chinese people lead an exercise, which they are good at. All of them can touch their toes. A man from Honduras says his shoulder hurts so bad, he can only watch, and one of the Oriental people gives him a back rub. They all seem to be good friends, and Rosa smiles at them and laughs over not being able to quite reach her toes.

Walking home, she's pleased with herself. This time she will try harder. She hopes they have time for the "do" and "did," what with all the exercising. No one in her life has ever asked Rosa to touch her toes, she thinks.

But she will keep up her attendance. Rosa doesn't know how this happened, but she has come to know important, high people: like the doctor daughter, and Gina, who was married to an opera singer in Italy, and Wolfie, who was a famous lawyer, and Mrs. Rose, who entertained the president of Venezuela once, and Winnie, who was very high in her way of talking even if she was crazy, and even Priscilla, whose ancestors built the mill on Moody Street...

...and she riding around on that bicycle and changing people's diapers, says Mrs. Fahey, as if Priscilla ought to give up her social position to someone more respectable, like herself.

X.
Mondo

Rosa thinks of all the times Mondo has returned from places he was sent to correct his ways; the drug program during junior high, the mental floor at the hospital when he was fifteen, then the juvenile detention the next year... Each time she was happy and hopeful. She wanted her Mondo back. Not this time. She is tired and discouraged, and it has been a relief not to worry about him. It would be good if he could go back to high school and get his education; but the school has forgiven all his lapses and given him a diploma two years ago. We should have given it back. Even though he spent six years in the high school, making up some classes, he didn't earn it, she thinks now. Eva was ready to march over and throw it in their faces, but Rosa had been too chagrinned at Mondo's mischief: the stolen video cameras, the defaced walls...

What Mondo wanted, his most ambitious aspiration, was to hang over overpasses and paint graffiti. The school allowed him once to paint a wall beside the walkway where the old Embassy Theater used to stand. Something community-minded, they wanted, but Mondo painted a picture so full of violence that it had to be painted out. As soon as his latest probation is over, he told her he wants to go to New York and challenge the real graffiti artists. This town, even Boston, is not a place that he can do his best, most daring work. He alarms her even more than his father did.

It's been two weeks since she's been at work. Monday she goes to Gina and takes the baby. It is a happy four hours. They chase him around and talk baby talk to him and to each other. *El nene, il bambino. Corre bambino, tan precioso el nene. Como que camina! Camina!* By lunchtime they are exhausted, and seat him between them, dipping biscuits into their *latte* to offer him, along with little bites of chicken salad and the yellow rice Rosa has brought.

XI.
She Speaks to Wolfie

Wednesday, she's back at the day center with Winnie. Wolfie is there. She has determined the next time there's an opportunity she will speak to him, but at first she can't even look at him. Suppose the Fahey woman sees her talking to him and reports her. Suddenly she's sure that will happen. She will lose her job and have to live on Max and Lidia's earnings. She's panicked and looks wildly around the room, breathing fast.

Then she's held. Her eyes are held fast by his. He is looking at her, the dear man. She forces her breathing to slow. She forces her eyes away from his until she is calm. Then she looks back. Still he is looking at her. She smiles then, and he smiles back, but his eyes are so sad.

So sad. Has he suffered? Of course he must have suffered. She has suffered. She must go to him. Courage comes. She stands and crosses the room. His wheelchair is pulled up at a table with Terry Fratus, Berta Bechtel, and some other silent people who are new to her. No one dares talk in Terry's presence. Berta is playing with a doll she was given for Christmas. Always Rosa used to place him with Mrs. Rose, who tried to make dinner table conversation and had interesting things to say.

She talks to him softly so that Mike won't shush her. I've been away, she tells him. My husband die. We find him in the river. He was sitting on a rock, smoking. It must be his heart.

More words than she had ever spoken to Wolfie, mistaking, before, his lack of voice with a lack of hearing.

There is his hand stretched out, his hand that has gravely explored her everywhere, everywhere. But she doesn't take it, for suddenly she is afraid. I must go back to Winnie, she says, but stays, unable to think of something to say.

But as she must say something, or leave, she blurts out, We roast a goat for Christmas... then she thinks, what a ridiculous thing to say.

In my country that is what we prepare for the holiday, she adds. It is important to say holiday rather than Christmas to Jews, she has heard. He is nodding, so she goes on.

My daughter is come, and she is almost a colonel. Of course I am proud of her.

He smiles. Oh, the dear man!

I hope you was having a happy holiday, she says, by way of ending the conversation, before people notice. Now I must leave.

As she backs away she has a glimpse of the keyboard and the screen pushed aside so that his lunch can be put in front of him. It has letters and little pictures. Is he learning to use the letters? She must ask Priscilla. There will be time for that, she thinks. She is pleased with her conversation now, in spite of the mention of the barbaric goat roast. Next time she will do better. It occurs to her that maybe Wolfie will like to hear some of the things she told Esmeralda.

XII.

An A+

Esmeralda has turned in her little biography of Rosa and has received an A+. The paper is to be read at a parents' open house at her school. Rosa must come.

But I be so embarrassed! she says.

She must go, however. No one will know who she is, that she is the woman in the biography. She could be someone's grandmother.

My teacher, Miss Sutherland, gave me a typewriter. She says I am a writer and I should practice as much as I can, Esmeralda tells Rosa in Rosa's kitchen.

My mother wants me to give it back; but I told her it's not a new typewriter. It was used by Miss Sutherland until she got her new word processor. So my mother say okay, and we gave Miss Sutherland a new Mexican blanket from the store.

Rosa knew how Mexicans, if you give them something, rush out to give you something back, and you can never be the last one to give them a gift. Unless you happen to die right after your last gift.

I so proud of you, Rosa says. I never hear of a teacher like that.

I love her, Esmeralda says. All the girls love her. We want Mr. Logan, the principal, to ask her to marry him. They are both so good-looking.

I once love my teacher, Rosa says. Her name was Señora Fiorini. She come from Argentina, and she have a little baby with gold hair like an angel. She bring him to school once. Once we rode some bicycles about twenty mile to visit her. It was a surprise. She so surprised and she give us lemon cake.

You didn't tell me that so I could put it in my biography, Esmeralda says.

I didn't tell you a lot of things, Rosa laughs.

It's hard for a writer to earn a lot of money, Miss Sutherland told me, but I can be a teacher too, and write in my spare time, she says.

And what will you write? Rosa asks, astounded at this development.

Biographies, I think. But there are a lot of things I haven't tried yet, like autobiographies.

What is that?

That's when you write about yourself.

Oh…

I'm waiting till I live a little more longer. I haven't fallen in love with a boy yet even.

Ah, Rosa says. That is a big *asunto*…

Did you love Mondo's father? You never told me that.

I love him terrible…

A lot?

Too much.

Why?

He no good. I never tell you that. I hide it from you.

Did you ever love anyone good?

Rosa gets tears in her eyes before she can answer.

Yes, she says. I love someone good...

It is Don Laureano, of course.

Now she's caught. She thinks of the little girl's gift—like Alejandro's gift—and is moved to tell the truth.

Not Don Laureano. Her eyes are filled to spilling over.

What must the little girl think? But she is a writer as well as a little girl. The teacher has told her to practice. And she knows so much...

I do love Don Laureano. He is my husband and I always serve him, Rosa says. But is someone else.

Can you tell me?

Rosa takes some moments of silence to think about this. Little Michael is jumping up and down under the shelf with the cookie jar. She thinks how Laureano loved to sit in this kitchen with the little girl and her notebook, drinking coffee and eating Goya biscuits, wanting to tell his stories too. Oh, Laureano was sweet man sometimes, she thinks sadly.

When you are sixteen, I will tell you, she says. She will tell her about Alejandro's badness, she thinks, and her craziness, maybe save her from some crazy love Esmeralda is having then; and she will tell her then about Wolfie. So she can know sixteen years old won't be her last crazy love...that there will be at least one more. Rosa gets up to bring down the cookies from the highest shelf, the only one Michael can't climb to: *Coja, mi amor.* She gives him two cookies. And you will have more words then, you know more words to 'splain it, she says to the little writer.

You mean I will be in love then.

Probably yes, says Rosa, feeling very wise and sad too. Probably you be in love!

She sits with Doña Marta, Esmeralda's mother, at the parents' open house at one of the small tables of the Roosevelt School third-grade room. She is blushing the whole time of Esmeralda's report. Her people are dark, but they can blush. *Chapas* are what the children of the high altitude's flaming cheeks are called. She sits in the little chair with burning *chapas* for all to see. She tries not listening, looking around at the displayed third-grade drawings; she tries the stoic pose of her people, sitting at the curb, waiting for buses. But nothing helps.

You look like a bride, Marta tells her.

I can no help it. Everybody know.

There is a certificate given, and the little girl looks right at her as she receives it. Rosa hopes she won't bring it to her; she doesn't, she brings it to her mother.

XIII.
Pick an Apple

Rosa goes two days a week to the English classes. She can touch her toes now, and the Chinese students laugh. The do's have come up, but not the did's, and Rosa wonders if maybe she should have tried harder in the test and dared to go to the intermediate class. Finally she asks Miss Ann Marie, and the teacher says, Oh, talking about yesterday ... We will take that up next month. So Rosa is patient, and practices saying to people, "How do you like I wash you back?" and "What do you like I make for supper?"

There is a new exercise called "pick an apple," in which you reach up and pretend to pick a fruit.

I pick an apple once in Billerica, Rosa tells Miss Ann Marie. I pick thousands of apples.

This brings on a premature discussion of "talking about yesterday, or last week or last year, or even earlier today."

You must say "picked," Rosa.

Pick.

Picked. Miss Ann Marie writes it on the blackboard. Ah, thinks Rosa, she should just give up now maybe.

We will practice, practice practice these past words soon, I promise, says the teacher. Let's all say this one now:

We picked apples last year.

We picked apples last year.

We picked apples last month.

We picked apples last week, they all say in chorus.

That is the past tense, says Miss Ann Marie. But we won't be scared of it. Mrs. Palumbo talked about the past tense all the time, which was what scared them all about ever passing to intermediate. This was the first time Miss Ann Marie has said the feared word. A woman from Iran asks about the "imperfect," and the teacher says, We won't be scared of that either. We will just say them over and over too. Out Loud.

Out Loud, they all say Out Loud.

Thousands of times, thinks Rosa, reassured.

I picked thousands of apples, Rosa says Out Loud, sure no one there can even comprehend what it is to pick thousands of apples.

Good, Rosa, says Miss Ann Marie.

XIV.
A Thorough Cleaning

Helen Schade is in the hospital. You can straighten up, they tell her at the agency. Just pick up a bit. We know she's messy.

Messy! Rosa bites her tongue. They are sure that a couple hours will do it. Remember we're not a cleaning agency, she is told.

When she come back? She asks.

Possibly not till next month.

Good... She is going to clean that house no matter what they say.

She buys a half gallon of Pine Sol, a large box of leaf bags, and some new mops and scrapers; then doesn't see how she can take all this on the bus. She asks Mondo if any of the cars that he's working on run.

What do you mean? They all run.

Then you can take me out to Piety Corner, she tells him.

He drops her off the next day at seven in the morning. She has the whole day to do as she pleases in this house. It is brutal work. First she must clear the loads of paper, supermarket flyers, coupons, old bills, mostly unpaid. These she puts aside to take to the agency. Already the electricity and the phone seem to have been turned off. The furnace is still roaring however. The law doesn't let you turn people's heat off that easily, she knows. Under all the paper is a layer of smaller things, coins, cigarettes, pills, and under that a layer of muck that causes everything to stick to the floor so that it is impossible to sweep it up into a dustpan.

Her hips begin to ache from bending over, so she decides to crawl around and throw everything into a plastic sheet. It is so unsanitary that she decides to throw away all the coins along with the loose pills. There are literally hundreds of pills in all shapes and colors. Helen's probably back in the hospital because of not taking them.

By noon, she has the bare linoleum floor of the breakfast nook and kitchen exposed; so she heaves herself up and sprays a layer of Pine Sol on it. Now a little rest before she scrubs and mops. She puts on a kettle of water for tea—luckily it's a gas stove—and toasts a muffin she's brought over the flame, allowing herself to sit at the scrubbed table she's cleared of Helen's coffee cups. The smell of Pine Sol always makes her think of home, of her aunt. People in this country are very smart and rich, she thinks; but, compared to the people of her country, they don't know what is clean. Twenty of her people, even twenty Guatemalans, could live in this house, and it would be neat and clean, even though they all worked. This was a surprising truth Rosa had seen for herself over the years. Her people also bathed more often than these, she suspected.

After throwing some water on the floor, she is able to take a push brush and move all the gunk into the dustpan. Now she can see the flower pattern in blue and green of the old linoleum; here and there it is torn and the wood floor exposed. After three moppings and changes of water, it is clean. One room. By the time she has set around twenty full bags of paper and junk out to the curb it is four o'clock. Next week she'll do the living room, which Helen barely used, and the downstairs bedroom, all littered with piles of dirty clothes. A satisfying day.

XV.
Mondo

She doesn't see him much. He has a job he goes to three days a week. She sees him get up and shower and go off at six o'clock. Then Fridays he goes to some kind of a therapy group and to visit his probation officer. So this much is good. But the other two days and the weekends he goes somewhere unknown, after waking up late and without showering.

Now he's telling her they want to take a piece of a wall he painted in Dorchester and put it in a museum...

How can they do that?

They use a mason's saw. What do I know! Graffiti art they call it. Art, that's what they called Alejandro's boat, she recalls.

Art! he shouts. It ain't art. It's a message! And it ain't new even. I do better work now.

What do you mean a message?

Oh, I can't explain it to you. He looks at her as if she isn't even a distant relative.

I am your mother. You don't remember?

Oh, I remember.

You listen to me. You father make something once they call art, and want to help him, want to give him an order for more boats just like it, and have him work for someone big, and he just like you. He want to make whatever comes in his head and not make when he feels like it, and they should leave him alone. And now you, his son, you talkin' just like him just so you can come to nothin' just like him.

Yeah, they call it Art and you gotta do it now, paint it now on a piece of plywood they can carry around and hang on walls. "A smaller scale" they want ... and they don't even know what it say ...

What it say?

It some old message. I don't even remember what alphabet I use then. I have a whole bran' new one I use now that I make up in the prison. And I don't work Dorchester no more, and I don't paint on no plywood ...

She has no idea what he's talking about and is about to walk out of the room when she remembers the wonders Esmeralda told her about the old tribes.

What alphabet? What are you talking about?

Messages. I can say fuck you, without no fucking eff and no fucking yoo and no fucking cee ... It ain't no fucking "art design" I'm making.

Well, how can it be a message without no ABC?

You thinking this ABC the only alphabet in the world? He looks at her swamp of ignorance.

No, she remembers Esmeralda telling her of old writings they only just in these days, thousands of years later, they figure it out.

But you make new ABC, who can read it? Only you ...

My people read it, they read my messages all over here, all over other cities.

But why must you hang youself over a bridge to write?

You think my people pay to go in *a museum* to read my message? The low down messages ain't no one read. It got to be up high! It got to be dangerous! With this he stumped out of the kitchen, went out in the yard and fired up one of his wrecks.

I guess you want to go live in the prison another year, she says after him, remembering how this argument about Art had gone differently with Alejandro: he opposed her; he wasn't going to try to make boats for the museum people, or the business people—she forgets which—but he wasn't going to make more boats for anybody, not even for himself, or do anything dangerous. He was just going to swing in the hammock and strum his guitar. Mondo is a better man, she thinks—in spite of the fear that she can feel like a lump in her throat as she goes about making the yellow rice.

She invites him to take her Saturday to Priscilla's apartment to paint the signs for the strike. They go in one of his wrecks and stop to pick up empanadas at the Mexican store for a treat. He wears a clean T-shirt and looks as handsome as Alejandro ever did, she thinks as they enter Priscilla's living room, which is full of people sitting on the floor with piles of poster board and bottles of paints around them.

She takes a chance and introduces Mondo to Priscilla as an artist who will be in a museum. Mondo laughs at this and walks off goofily; but Priscilla says, Really?

Yes, it's true, Rosa says. He paints letters.

But that's wonderful! Priscilla goes after him and asks him to be the one person sitting at her small dining table blocking out in pencil the signs that say:

HEALTH WORKERS UNITE

WE CARE FOR YOUR LOVED ONES

A LIVING WAGE FOR NURSES AIDES

PAY US WHAT WE DESERVE

ONE FOR ALL

UNIONS NOW

He doesn't need a pencil, picks up a brush instead and turns them out so fast that the people on the floor are put to stapling the finished boards to the pieces of lathe that Priscilla had them cut for her at the lumberyard.

Wow! says Priscilla's son Frostie, standing behind Mondo.

I can make them fancier, he offers.

No, no, Priscilla says. They should look like we did them ourselves. People are going to think we hired an advertising agency as it is.

What a kid, Priscilla says to Rosa after they're done. It's only eight-thirty and they're already drinking Mexican tamarindo sodas and eating the empanadas.

His father was an artist, Rosa confides softly to Priscilla so Mondo doesn't hear. He carved a boat that was in a museum in Tegucigalpa.

Rosa is home by four on Thursday. She starts the rice and heats the milk for a cup of coffee.

She misses Laureano all of a sudden. He would come in grinning and tell her to make another cup. Now she sits alone. She wishes Lidia would come home early and set little Michael on the floor. Laureano's children she can understand, even the twins have girlfriends now, who will tame them. She simply cannot understand her own. She fears for them in a way she could never fear for her stepchildren. They don't want normal things. Even Eva, when she called her last week and Rosa asked her how was Deroy, told her he was over, that the difference in their rank had come between them. At Eva's age you were supposed to fall in love and become blind to everything else. Eva will probably never marry, she thinks now; it isn't in her plans. And who would marry a graffiti artist who hangs over bridges at three in the morning to paint fuck you in a new language?

There will be no grandchildren for her, she must accept it.

But then she thinks of little Michael and Esmeralda and cheers up. It isn't just your own you need to have happiness in. And then Lidia comes in and asks if the milk is still hot, and Rosa is up on her legs doing again and back to herself.

XVI.
Spring Songs

Some days come along like days in spring. Even the bird songs sound like spring songs, different from winter songs, she couldn't say why—February's teasing. Buds swell up on her laurel bushes.

Priscilla tells her that Terry, at the agency, is dying of his kidney disease. They must find him a donor this month or it will be too late. Meanwhile they are all giving blood for him if they can. Rosa's is the wrong type; but they take it to restore one of the pints that Terry's used from the blood bank. Priscilla takes her after work on Thursday to see him. He doesn't know how bad it is, Priscilla tells her, so don't look so gloomy.

Terry is sitting up beside his bed, looking not so hot, Rosa notes. He's grown a big red beard, springy and curly and healthy looking, which seems to have taken all the life out of the limp hair on his head and his frail body. Rosa daydreams while he and Priscilla talk union matters.

Why had the attempt last year failed? Priscilla thinks it is because it was too hard to leave people like Winnie and Clifford and Wolfie to their own devices, and three of them, including Rosa, had snuck off to work. Terry and Priscilla had taken all of them to the Sunshine Club and left them there, which Rebecca didn't appreciate. This time they have assigned people to help Rebecca. They knew from last time the invalids were mostly sent to the hospital while families pitched in for the others. They could have waited this out. Hospital stays were expensive. There would have been pressure on the agencies from the hospital if they had just waited. Another reason they went back, Rosa knows, was because they were hurting for two weeks without pay, so this time there was a fund, 5 percent of each month's earnings had been donated since last October. This time, Priscilla is saying, everyone is prepared to go a month. There is the fund, and there will be some money from the unions to help out with groceries and such. And as for Rebecca, she has a big salary and should stand with them in spite of the aggravation; a stay in the hospital won't harm anyone, and the hospital has its own union. Yeah, let them stand with us, Terry shouts, as if this strike was the only worry on his mind.

They've pulled him through so many times he just thinks this is another little setback, Priscilla tells her as they leave. I'd like to tell him the truth, but his wife wants to keep it from him.

Rosa feels bad. Terry used to care for Wolfie before he got so sick, and Wolfie always looked sleek and well back then. He looks nothing like that now.

PART THREE

I.
Rosa Speaks

Two days go by, and she doesn't see Wolfie. Then, on Monday, he is there again. He looks ill. His food sits in front of him untouched. The Fahey woman has tried to feed him and given up.

Filthy man, Rosa hears her say to Mrs. Rose.

What has he done?

Has he had his hands under the Fahey woman's blouse?

Rosa can't help the thought. It sickens her.

No, he wouldn't! she tells herself. She's moved across the room and stands in front of the Fahey woman.

What he do?

S'matter with you?

What he do?

What you talking about?

Wolfie. What he do, you call him filthy?

Filthy man …

What he do? She fears the answer.

Disgusting …

What?

Crap his pants. Just clean him up and he does it again.

She's flooded with relief.

He knows better, filthy man!

Of course he knows better. He's sick, you bad woman! He's sick!

The rest of the day Rosa couldn't tell you what she was at. The work gets done somehow: Winnie returned to Leo, changed and put to bed, a load of Clifford's wash put in and washed and dried, while she straightens up the parts of the apartment he lets her touch.

She arrives at the agency ten minutes before it closes. Janet is there with Mrs. Hingy, smoking a cigarette, and studying the takeout menu from the Waltham House of Pizza.

Rosa stands in the doorway to the conference room and begins without prelude.

Why you not send me to Wolfie no more?

Janet drops her cigarette into her coffee cup. What?

What that woman say about me? Rosa adds. She is choked with anger.

The two women look at each other, genuinely puzzled.

What woman, Rosa?

That Fahey woman, what she tell you? Rosa is sure now of the woman's malice.

Janet, who is nicer than Mrs. Hingy, looks at her with concern.

Nothing, Rosa. What are you talking about?

She say I do something wrong with Wolfie…

Janet is shaking her head. Nothing, Rosa, we don't understand.

Then why you not send me?

Rosa, you are illegal. You know that we don't hire illegals, don't you? It's taking a chance… and Wolfie is a lawyer.

The fact of her common-law marriage, of Wolfie's inability to talk, crowd into her thoughts, but her enormous relief pushes these thoughts away.

If you don't send me to him, I quit, she blurts out.

But why, Rosa? We don't want you to quit.

These kind words are making her cry now, and she's not capable of any more explaining. In a minute she'll confess that she loves Wolfie, and that won't do; so she simply gives in to tears and speechlessness.

Of course we'll send you back, Rosa, she hears through her laments. We don't want you to quit. But you must not tell Wolfie you're illegal.

No, no, she wails, and I not illegal. I am married to Puerto Rican man, fourteen years...

Well, why don't you fix your papers, then?

I not know. It common law. I not know.

But never mind that; she must get back to Wolfie. He could die of the Fahey woman's cruelty any day now.

We are doing a new schedule. Beginning next month we'll put you on.

Oh, thank you, thank you, she cries, then controls herself and runs out. What will they think!

Well, her English has all gone to hell now, Rosa thinks Sunday as she walks through her side garden, picking off the *flores marchitas* from her roses. She throws these on her compost pile and proceeds down to the river. Max has repaired Laureano's boat and is out in the middle, fishing. A nice recreation for him, Rosa thinks. She can't think of any other pleasure he gives himself.

Her verbs went all to hell the moment she confronted the Fahey woman over her calling Wolfie a filthy man.

Mrs. Fahey considers all her patients filthy, bothersome, pieces of shit, so why should this have set her off so . . . ?

Then she remembers her first thought on hearing this had been that maybe Wolfie had touched the Irish woman. A truly shocking thought. How could she think it!

"Sooner kiss a mackerel" were Alcide's words to her one day about that woman. Alcide had an eye for women, a French eye, Rosa thought of it.

That was it.

Wolfie had an eye too. A Jewish eye. A worshipful eye . . .

Rosa is sure Wolfie has never heard of the Virgin. But it was almost as if somewhere in his imagination She lived, some notion of her . . .

The Virgin's beauty and also her goodness.

Wolfie must be completely familiar by now with all of the Fahey woman's shortcuts and impatience; she hopes not too much about her cruelty . . .

Impossible he doesn't.

She knows Wolfie's dead wife must have been a beautiful, good woman who gave him two fine sons.

Her memory wanted him to worship Woman, Woman in the shape of Rosa.

. . . Ooman.

Not the shape of the Fahey woman with her dining-room-table legs and her bulky shoulders. A freckled toad, Alcide calls her. Sooner would he kiss a freckled toad . . .

She has freckles even on her eyelids, Rosa has noted.

She is convincing herself.

And would the Fahey woman ever notice Wolfie's beauty?

His unblemished skin. Like the unblemished calf required for sacrifice.

Of course it was the shock. Anyone would lose their verbs.

Rosa forgives herself.

She goes back over all her *disparates.*

What he do? Addressed to Mrs. Fahey.

She should have said, What did he do? Even though the Fahey woman didn't even deserve the effort.

The effort was for Ann Marie, she tells herself.

But such a shock!

Maybe it was a lucky thing, because it caused Rosa to lose something else besides her verbs: her fears ... and sent her right over to the agency, where she should have gone long ago ...

Why you not send me to Wolfie no more?

This one requires some thinking about.

Why do you ...?

Why do you not send ...?

Finally she brings it up in the class. *Porque no me manda ahora?* She has to say it to Michelle, who is from Haiti and knows Spanish; then Michelle can say it in French or something to Ann Marie, who is also from Haiti; and Ann Marie looks kindly at Rosa's befuddled face and says: "Why don't you send me, anymore?" and says it in French to the other Haitians, and they say it in French to some people from Vietnam, and one of these can say it in Chinese to Chang, who is a friend of Mrs. Rose's, and can say it in Russian to the two Russians. This leaves out only the Iranian lady, so they are all laughing at their cleverness, even Ann Marie, who is shaking her head and protesting: We aren't supposed to do this ...? Rosa remembers Mrs. Polumbo scolding, Only English in this classroom, whenever some people wanted to say something in their own language.

And then, in pretend punishment, the whole class has to practice:

Why don't you send me anymore...?

Why don't you eat that...?

Why don't you eat that spinach?

Ten times each. And: Anymore, anymore, anymore, anymore, anymore...

Anymore, anymore, anymore, anymore... Rosa practices on the way to Piety Corner, where hardly anyone, anyone, anyone... passes to note her talking to herself Out Loud.

Why don't you send me anymore, why don't you send me anymore, why don't you send me anymore...

II.
The Strike

Priscilla invites Mondo to the house to create one gorgeous sign. Just so you can read it, she says, and offers him an extra large piece of poster board and his choice of slogans.

WE CARE FOR YOUR

LOVED ONES

He does it in four DayGlo colors. It is beautiful, with colors you didn't know existed, colors that have no names Rosa knows. Like modern paintings she sees in Gina's house.

What happens if you win this strike? he asks Rosa.

We get more pay. Part-time get some benefits.

He is thoughtful.

You like Priscilla, right? asks Rosa.

Yeah. She try to tell me how important are unions. Talkin' about Cesar Chavez.

Rosa is careful. Can I tell you something I think of the other day?

Sure.

I think you gonna be better man than you father.

That jerk!

He is in a museum once too.

Mentira.

It's true. He carved a boat.

Yeah…

Then they want him to make another one like it. Do some kind of business with them. He don't want to do it. He think they just using him.

Prob'ly they was.

Priscilla, is she using you?

Sure.

But you let her…

Well, I can dig unions maybe.

So, you a better man than you father. I can respect you.

What you talkin' about? You think I should go makin' union signs the rest of my life.

No, Rosa says. Only sometimes. Like to stay in this family…you do…something this family can understand.

Well, maybe. But I got my own work to do.

That's okay. Your father, when they tell them what they want, he say no. But then he never say like you, I got my own work. He lay in the hammock and swing…

Okay, he nods, I read you, Mama. He gets up then and kisses her and walks out of the kitchen with his goofy walk, picking up little Michael on the way and turning him upside down.

Mondo.

Me purifica. She has to laugh.

Everything is about the strike lately, but in the back of Rosa's mind is the delicious thought of going to Wolfie.

She hasn't felt this way since she was nineteen and in love with Alejandro. Counting days, counting minutes. Planning how it will be. What she will say to him.

She is planning to tell Wolfie about Esmeralda. Hearing about Esmeralda will make him proud of the things he did to help people get legal and get out of trouble. And about Eva the colonel. Did she ever tell him about Eva? She will tell him also about her common-law marriage that she was ignorant of for fifteen years, and ask him for advice, which will make him interested in his keyboard so he can answer her. He will feel like he is back at work and important again. In his office with his coat and tie. When the bookmobile comes she will get him books the way Priscilla used to do for Megan. She would read to him if she could, but that would embarrass her. Maybe she can read the book at the same time as he is reading it... while he naps perhaps. He must nap, and eat good food. She will bring him soup, and wash his hair with protein soap so he becomes sleek and handsome again. His son will see a difference in him, and won't take away the expensive machine. And they will talk about the things in the books they read, and about the things that Esmeralda is studying in her fourth grade. She hopes they won't seem childish to him. She will ask Priscilla, or Mrs. Rose, what should she talk about. Mrs. Rose entertained the president of Venezuela once, at her hacienda.

He isn't at the Sunshine Club Tuesday when she brings Winnie in and seats her by Mrs. Rose, who is trying to have a conversation with Asa Babcock about West Boylston, where they both had lived back in the Thirties, and Asa tells again the story of the opal that fell from her brooch that she stuck back with a drop of pitch. And Mrs. Rose tells Asa Babcock about how she and her big brother used to mix up stolen cleaning liquids and kitchen leftovers and stuff they found in the garage in order to make an explosion, or make gold or something ... and Terry Fratus tells them to stop talking, crikey; and Mrs. Rose tells him she thought the Irish liked stories ...

But not the same ones over and over, my dear woman.

No Irish Need Apply, Winnie shouts.

Rosa hopes he's just late, but lunchtime comes and goes and still no Wolfie. The Fahey woman isn't there. She is at his apartment killing him, Rosa fears suddenly.

Rosa hasn't bled since just before Christmas. So it's over, she thinks: the tender breasts, the heavy womb, the alarming bleeding ... But on Friday night she dreams she is lying in a hammock and Alejandro is touching her all over. It is so real that she wakes with a start and finds herself on the point of coming ... so close she must take the sheets and bunch them between her legs and bring herself the rest of the way, something she hasn't done since she was a girl. She isn't finished with it after all, she finds, feeling again the ache in the breasts and the heavy womb. She checks the bed to see if it's started, but nothing. She thinks it starts later in the day while she's making Clifford's bed, but nothing. The pains are bad while she's finishing up the cleaning of Helen Schade's house, but she ignores them. No woman's the boss of her body, she thinks. Wolfie will find her in the same state as he left her.

He's at the Sunshine Club Monday, so that's a relief. She's on the schedule to go to him in two weeks, on Thursday, her old day. The strike is to start next Monday. If they are still on strike in two weeks, she will go anyway, without logging in her hours, she thinks.

He's there on Friday, doesn't touch his food. Priscilla's with him, coaxing, so Rosa doesn't worry. It starts to snow, so they all go home early.

III.

A Spring Storm

The streets are already covered and only the tips of the grass showing, and it's almost as black as midnight when Rosa gets the bus.

She can see the grass is long covered, and the mailboxes have mailbox-shaped mounds building up on them as she walks the three blocks from the bus stop to her home.

Max has cleared their walk, but it was a while ago, before he went to his second job, so it is piling up again, but not quite over the tops of her shoes.

No one is home and nothing's going on the stove, so she takes some lentils she has soaking and cooks them with some chopped tomatoes and onions, and puts the rice on to boil. They'll be glad to have it when they come home. Just when the rice is done, Esmeralda comes in with little Michael. Her mother and father have gone to Leominster for eggs and got stuck on the highway, she says.

What will they do?

Once when it was bad like this they had to sleep in the back of the truck.

You stay here. We'll have these lentils. She adds a can of lunch meat cut into cubes, and some carrots and spinach, more canned tomatoes. One of her aunt's *solo platos.*

Lidia comes in. Her boss has brought her home. After they eat, Rosa puts little Esmeralda to bed on the couch. The lights are coming on and off, and, oddly, there is thunder, like a summer storm. It snows through the night. Max comes in at two, and an hour later she wakes again to hear the muffled sound of the plows and the flashing red lights on the ceiling.

In the morning Max and Mondo are up before anyone, digging what is now almost a tunnel out to one of Mondo's cars and a wider swath to the street. The strike is called off. Only doctors and nurses are allowed on the roads that run between house-high piles left by the plows. Esmeralda's sisters come for her. Their parents won't be home anytime soon. Let her stay here, Rosa says, and gives the sisters some coffee.

Rosa lets the goats come in the kitchen. Little Michael loves the goats. He is a goat, he insists. He eats from a dish on the floor like the goats, and butts heads with Blanca, who has grown to be a bit bigger than he is and can back him into corners. Finally the two of them trip Rosa as she's filtering the coffee and she screams: *Jesús, Maria, y José! Que salgan de aquí!*

Esmeralda takes him and the goats out to play in the tunnel. She digs him a place to sit halfway out to Mondo's car. It is a throne. He is a king. A king of goats.

The agency calls at one. Nurses' aides are allowed to drive on the streets. There are no buses, but if she can get around in a car, she must get to her consumers. Carry her agency card in case she's stopped.

Mondo, thrilled to be on the road, takes her downtown. She sees people skiing down the middle of Moody Street. He drops her at the sisters'. She can walk to the others.

Winnie won't have a bath today. It's too cold. It's eighty in here, Leo says.

Rosa puts on the bathroom heater; nice and warm, nice and warm. We'll leave the girdle on.

An epic day, Winnie says.

The storm you mean.

A coronation! And I am to attend.

Ah, we'll dress you in something nice, Rosa says, pulling off Winnie's nightgown and quickly wrapping her shoulders in a towel and coaxing her onto the bath chair. There is no Sunshine Club today. Leo will have to play rummy all day. He is in the study with two TVs on, deep into the weather reports. An epic storm, she hears through the wall.

We sisters were at the Mother's coronation. We all had pillbox hats, and organdy flounces. We were given certificates from the Old King for our lacework in 1913. That is why we were invited.

Rosa checks beneath the girdle. The skin is healthy again, only slightly flushed from the heat. She is sweating and tries to switch off the heater, but Winnie catches her at it: Ye've put the penny in it, woman, so let us have all the heat we're due.

Okay, okay. Winnie's feet and lips are blue. Her toenails are yellow crumbs.

The daughter is nothing to the Mother. A little low creature, says Winnie.

Which daughter is that? Rosa asks.

Our Queen, shouts Winnie. The Queen is dead, long live the Queen.

Oh, says Rosa, what was her name?

Ye're obviously an ignorant woman, Winnie crows.

Okay, says Rosa, crushed. Winnie's speech is as sharp as her elbows. She's tempted to leave off her painstaking sponging under the girdle and bring this bath to an end. The late start means she'll have a time getting to all of them as it is.

The Glorious Elizabeth ... Winnie says, like she's reading from a poem. She knew how to handle men. That was another Elizabeth.

Oh, you mean Queen Elizabeth, Rosa says. I used to have a postcard with a picture of her on a pony.

She dries and powders Winnie liberally, then pulls on her undershirt, getting a poke in the ribs for her effort to be firm but gentle as the agency counseled. Then the housedress and the heavy stockings, working them over the crumbly toenails.

Walking to Clifford's, right down the middle of Myrtle Street, a doctor on skis, who took out Eva's tonsils, smiles and lifts a pole. Doctor Massessa, she remembers his name. He used to call Eva "The Princessa." The medical community, only the medical community is allowed to be out and around, the newsman said on Channel 5. They were supposed to be out here striking today. Even some of the doctors were planning to support them, Priscilla said, and some of the nurses. The medical community. It has a nice sound. She hopes Mondo went straight home. Without her in the car he is illegal on the road. Well, what does he care about illegal? She wonders sometimes if Mondo could commit a real crime, something that didn't involve a wall or a bridge. She used to fear he could; now she thinks it's less likely. That doesn't mean he'll stay out of prison, however... Even Priscilla went to prison once for her speeches on Boston Common.

Rosa wonders about Wolfie. Maybe the Fahey woman will refuse to go and they'll have to send him to a nursing home, like during the last strike. He will be safe there. Maybe she'll have time to stop after she's through, just to check him. Just a friendly visit. She has to remind herself, still, that in the agency's eyes she is innocent, is supposed to be going back to him in nine more days. Unless the strike... the strike could last three weeks. That's what Terry and Priscilla planned for.

She will go to him anyway. What can they do to her? Put her in prison? She laughs. What kind of crime is it to disobey a union? They could just as well put her in prison for walking about with a sign on a pole. The union itself is illegal to some people. She stops and pulls up a sock inside her boot. These are difficult thoughts. She'll have to ask Priscilla. Where it is the law's opinion against Priscilla's, she will pick Priscilla. This thought comforts her. But if she goes to Wolfie, that would be going against Priscilla's strike. Well, not Priscilla's strike. It's not *my* strike, Rosa, it's ours, Priscilla had said to her more than once.

But they said we could help Rebecca, she recalls. They were not going to make people outside the strike suffer too much this time, she does remember hearing at the meetings.

She has to pull up the sock again. Why do some socks get sucked down this way and others not?

Well, Wolfie is outside the strike. The people assigned to help Rebecca the first few days are not to log in their hours. Of course, she can go to Wolfie without logging in. Mondo will carry her sign while she is with him. Mondo will be illegal; that will please him. She's sure he'll do it for her.

The snow-covered road is turning to ice. She slides along in her boots as if she's on skis, and slips and sits hard on her tailbone on the sidewalk in front of Clifford's apartment, gets up laughing, thinking of Mondo.

She thinks the fall will bring on the bleeding, the way a push from Alejandro landing her on her tail brought on Eva's birth. But nothing, just the dull cramp she's had for a week now.

IV.
Marching

It's nearly April already. The epic snow cannot last. It is dripping away. Dripping from the eaves; the pine boughs release it and spring back from their heavy loads. The rich green grass of Rosa's side yard shows here and there. Only the giant dirty mounds left by the plows remain by Thursday, when the strike is rescheduled to happen.

She reports to Priscilla's apartment. Her daughter Solie is passing out the signs. Solie is known to run around with Puerto Rican boys who are too old for her. This is a sorrow for Priscilla.

There is a Xeroxed schedule with assigned hours. Rosa is to start at noon; until then she and Enedina López can get consumers to the Sunshine Club and help Rebecca. No baths, no writing notes in the books; it is to seem as if they were never there.

She goes to Alcide, and here she loses all her militancy. The dear man is holding one of Eulalie's nightgowns and lying still in bed with tears standing in his eyes.

You go on strike. What I do? I have no woman. She kisses him. You have woman, Alcide. You have Priscilla and Enedina, and you have me.

He brightens. You come here in bed…

No!

No, no, you have to go marching, I know. He gets up and marches to a tune he hums into the bathroom to take a long pee. He is dressed, but very haphazardly. She tries to straighten him.

You a good woman, he says. You got your teeth? This is an encouraging sign. They thought he would just give up and die after Eulalie.

Yeah, I got most of my teeth, she laughs. She has lost two molars, but they're at the back and don't show.

You still bleed, too, I bet.

Rosa takes a deep breath, feeling her heavy womb. It still has not started. Yes, I bleed, Alcide.

That's good, he says. Keeps the juices in a woman.

She laughs and dances away from him, afraid he will touch her.

You suppose to go right to the Sunshine Club. No fooling around today.

Ah, yes. He wags his hips and marches in place, hup two, hup two. To the Bastille, *Allons garçons*.

She sets him moving toward the door. He looks terrible, but at least he has cheered up.

It's taken more time than she's allowed, and the van is waiting, impatient, outside.

They all look terrible at the day center. She'd like to take every one of them and give him a bath. But Rebecca is carrying on with the breakfast and the Reality Orientation, and Rosa and Enedina clear the paper plates they're using in place of dishes to allow the kitchen people their turn with the signs.

Good for you, Mrs. Rose says to Rosa. I always was a little *pink*, watching all those snooty Englishmen in India and those big company types my husband worked for.

Thank you, Rosa says, not understanding, wondering if this "pink" is somehow connected to Mrs. Rose's unusual pinkish hair.

If I could walk better, I'd be right out there with you. To the Bastille! she cries, like Alcide; and now Rosa must wonder what this Bastille is. She'll have to ask Esmeralda. There's no time to ask Mrs. Rose.

Then Mrs. Hingy from the agency turns up and tries to take things in hand. But everything is in hand, and Rebecca, who is very grim and calm, takes her into the kitchen and speaks sharply to her and puts her to help Rosa and Enedina take people to the bathroom. Rosa can see this doesn't please her. Rosa tries to avoid looking at her, afraid she might start apologizing for the strike. She's a little worried that they might take back their agreement about Wolfie.

Where is Wolfie? She imagines him waiting in his chair, needing to urinate, needing to eat. These were things they were supposed to be helping him to learn to do for himself, and no one of them ever worked on it with him. There wasn't time in the schedule for this, even though they all sat through boring workshops showing you how to teach people to stand by themselves in the toilet, holding the rails; and to prepare simple food from a wheelchair; and, even though Wolfie's kitchen was specially adapted for wheelchair cooking with low counters and refrigerator and stove he could reach, no one had ever got him to cook...

She is about to excuse herself and run to him when Priscilla comes in with him. He is holding one of Mondo's signs in his right hand and actually grinning. Priscilla tells her she left the strikers to check the consumers and discovered Mrs. Fahey had simply stayed home.

She tells me she wasn't in favor of the strike, Priscilla hisses in Rosa's ear.

She doesn't need benefits; her husband gives her everything she needs; she only works this job to keep herself busy, Priscilla says. All things Rosa's heard many times; she might have known this would happen.

So why she don't log in and go to her job? Rosa says.

Oh, she tells me she's afraid the strikers might injure her. Her husband told her to stay in the house, so that's what she's doing... I, myself, will injure her if she dares come out to go shopping, continues Priscilla, taking up her sign from Wolfie and kissing him for being a good sport.

Rosa is so proud of him. She gets him some of the toast and scrambled eggs that is left in the kitchen, and some good hot coffee, then takes him to sit by Mrs. Rose, bringing her some coffee as well.

Mr. Wolfe will like to hear about India and all, Rosa says.

Then she must go. It is after twelve, and the two strikers who are to relieve them have come in ten minutes ago.

Wolfie must learn to pee by himself and to cook. She is picturing this in her mind as she walks up Moody Street to find the strikers.

They are taking a break by an empanada vendor at the end of the Common where the railroad crossing is. The medical community, she thinks proudly. Frostie brings her an empanada. The doctors are paying, he tells her. Not all of them. There's a small group supporting us. You go by our apartment tomorrow and there'll be a check from the union.

That be nice. She is feeling *consentida*, the way she feels at Gina's ... tomorrow is her day at Gina's. She hasn't thought what to do about Gina yet. Fortunately she's finished Helen's house; otherwise this would be a bother hanging over her. Her mind goes over the scrubbed rooms, light and fresh and orderly. She wishes someone other than Helen was coming back to occupy it.

Frostie brings her some coffee and a sign which says:

A LIVING WAGE

She sits on a low wall and sips the coffee. The sun has some warmth in it now.

May first. Labor Day in Moscow and other places.

The real Labor Day, Priscilla told the strikers last night when they were making final preparations. It wasn't planned for this day, but it was a good day. An auspicious day, Priscilla said.

What other places? Rosa wanted to know. Well, Italy and France and Spain, she was told. Mediterranean places, she told herself, recalling the map in Laureano's atlas.

I put lots of sugar in your coffee, Frostie says. Some people, like my mom, can't drink it with even a grain of sugar in it; but Latino people like at least two spoonfuls, he says.

Such a nice boy. A noticing boy, she thinks; Priscilla has told her he gets to take college courses in high school. You going to be a union person like your mom? she asks.

In my spare time, maybe. I plan to be a scientist. Yes, I think I will be a union person. I never had much experience at it till lately. He pushes up his glasses exactly the way Priscilla does. I think everyone should be a union person.

A good boy, she thinks. How proud Priscilla must be.

She thinks of Eva and studies her sign:

A LIVING WAGE

Each letter is made with just a stroke or two of the brush.

Mondo.

Priscilla comes and sorts them into two groups: one group to return to Irons Street in front of the Sunshine Club, the other to walk on Moody in front of the agency, starting at the Waltham Spa and turning back when they get to Myrtle Street. Rosa is in this group.

Her womb drags at her when she starts out; but by the time she has walked a block she feels better. She's wearing a pad, just in case.

People are stopping on the opposite sidewalk. Some are clapping, others just watch. She sees the Kisser and the train girl with her flag. Rosa has to keep checking that her sign is turned the right way around. They pass the agency, which looks closed, and she thinks of Mrs. Hingy trying to pull down Winnie's panties: I'll not have any funny business with me panties, thank you very much! And of Mrs. Rose telling Wolfie about India and Venezuela. What was the thing she meant to ask Esmeralda about? She can't remember.

She sees herself march by in the windows of the Irish Travel Bureau. Is Wolfie thinking of me now, she wonders?

Of us, she corrects herself. The medical community.

Then sees herself again in the Red Rooster Café.

Oh, the Bastille, it was. Something French, she suspects. She used to ask Eulalie about this sort of thing. She could ask Alcide sometime, she supposes. When there's time... when there's ever time. She thinks of Eulalie in her grave, and then Laureano, and then her mother. Eulalie's body, ghastly flesh being eaten away, leaving the clean bones. Her mother must be nothing but bones now, and no one left in Xoyatla to tend her grave. Every one of them either dead or moved here, and no school for the children, or rather no children for the school.

They turn at the top of the hill and start down the opposite sidewalk. Rosa shifts her sign around. A policeman on a horse has shooed them off the sidewalk into the gutter, and a few pedestrians are shouting at them, but most are ignoring them, hurrying with shopping bags. A few are watching them, and a group of men and women has joined their march. From the Methodist church up the hill, someone tells her. She sees that Father Beauvais from Saint Charles is also being carried along, with a group of high school kids, it looks like. The Kisser has also joined them in his Red Sox uniform.

In front of the agency, Priscilla calls a halt. They are to shuffle around in tight circles on the curb. A small group of them is assigned to obstruct the entrance to make sure no new hires go in. It's Rosa's kind of people, illegals, they're afraid will get inside and take their jobs. A policeman on foot tries to move them along, but they hold firm. Rosa is continually stepping off from the curb and back up again. A traffic jam has formed, and impatient cars are heard from.

The people obstructing the agency's doors are jostled by two policemen now, but they are firmly sticking there. Rosa and the rest of them get moved along down toward the Common, but get themselves turned around and start back up.

But I'm not illegal, she reminds herself. This lovely thought is always ready to step up to the front of her mind. I'm not illegal. Let these policeman take me off to jail if they want.

Still, she must feel for these people she hears are eager to replace them. Their hardships tug at her. Is the union harming them? This question is too difficult to pursue while she's being shoved from behind and held back by the people in front of her.

At three o'clock Priscilla rallies them in the Common. She assigns people to keep the watch on the agency in shifts. Rosa's shift isn't until day after tomorrow. Those strikers not parading in front of the two agencies now on strike are to rally in the Common and to bring coffee and donuts to the people in front of the agencies, from eleven in the morning till four in the afternoon. Everyone must show up for at least the morning or the afternoon.

She hurts everywhere riding home on the bus. Lidia is kind and fixes supper while she sits in Laureano's recliner, which has become Rosa's; no one else ever sits in it. Were there fights, Mondo wants to know; did anyone hit you?

Nobody hit me, Rosa says. It wasn't a war. Just everybody pushes, and it hard to hold a sign up all the time.

You arms get so tired, and then it's up on the curb and down in the street and pushing, pushing.

The second day of the strike is similar to the first. Rosa sees some of her own people sitting around, but none of them attempt to enter the agency. They would be too afraid, Rosa thinks.

Alcide is not in the apartment. Rosa looks everywhere. His WalkAide seems also to be gone. Eulalie used to hide it, but no one bothers anymore, because he hasn't escaped in months. She should have been warned yesterday when he asked if she had all her teeth. During most of Eulalie's dying he stayed around moping. No one thought he might go back to his old ways. What to do?

She tries to think of places they used to find him: the little park where the Embassy used to be, Mama Josie's, the used car lot on Myrtle, the Gold Star Mothers Bridge where he used to hang over and look at the pilings where the dance hall was. If she goes to the Common by the long way round she can hit a couple of them, as Mondo would say. No way she can call the agency, or Priscilla.

She waves the van away and starts out.

You see Alcide? she asks Batty at the car lot.

Alcide? You mean Frenchy? We thought he was dead.

No, his wife, she die.

Not here, he says. We'll watch for him though. What you want us to do with him, give him a job or something?

No, keep him here. I'll try to be back.

Yes, ma'am. We'll do that.

She thanks them, then turns into the cemetery at the big old beech tree with the initials carved everyplace. He showed her once his and Eulalie's carved in its trunk.

They are high up now, where its boughs begin to spread. She looks up at the bank of the railroad tracks where the homeless men sit. No Alcide. Then she walks in, past the very old slate graves with the funny names and little stones for the children:

Born 1672, died 1673.

Another one lived a month:

Born January 1749, died February 1749.

Pity.

Then, moving on, the little granite houses with the spiked fences around, rich people. And at the very top of the hill, Italians, like Gina. Here are carved angels and Virgins, like graves at home. She supposes there is a French neighborhood somewhere. None of her own kind here.

It's a pretty place. The river edges in here and there among the reeds, which are full of birds and butterflies. *Mariposas*. She forgets about Alcide for a moment, would like to sit in the grass and think about places where her own are buried: her aunt, her mother...

Of course she can go in no farther. There's no time, so she walks back out. Then the bridge. No Alcide here either, only pigeons and an abandoned shopping cart. Mama Josie's is way the other way on Main Street. And so is O'Reilly's Daughter where he goes sometimes. Too far. She must find Priscilla.

Priscilla is among the people guarding the agency today. Standing by the familiar agency, with Alcide on her mind and only ten minutes before she must take up her sign, Rosa, for a moment, feels her allegiances all mixed up. Whose responsibility is Alcide?

The police, Priscilla tells her. One of the men down by the railroad crossing has a radio telephone. She must tell him to call the station.

Okay. I already look three places. She walks the rest of the way down the hill, sees it's not necessary to make any calls. Alcide has joined the strikers. He is sitting by the bus stop with a bunch of French-Canadian strikers talking French and ignoring her scolding.

They're feeding him hot dogs from one of the many carts that have taken to accompanying the strikers, so she leaves off worrying. He can take himself home, and if he does something illegal, like doing his *caca* in the streets, the police are sure to take him in. That was always Eulalie's hope—that they'd put him in the *calabozo*, instead of always bringing him home, so she could have some peace.

Ah, poor Eulalie, she have her peace now...Then Rosa worries about Wolfie. She imagines the agency making an arrangement with Mrs. Fahey to do all the baths, and paying her double. They could give her Rosa's consumers plus her own. She knows some of Mrs. Fahey's baths are pretty rough and hurried-up affairs so she can get back to putting her feet up and reading her magazine or listening to her police radio. If she has a double schedule, what will they be like? In, out, cold water, soap in the eyes...

She eats a hot dog and takes up her sign and patrols the Common with the others.

They're singing a song today that starts, Go Down Moses. Rosa sings these three words, but doesn't know the rest of them.

The meeting is at the Italian-American Hall instead of Priscilla's house that week, and there are a lot of unfamiliar people there. All the agencies are out now, and there are three people from the New York SEIU, Priscilla tells her. An important development.

Here she's given a paper with the words to "Go Down Moses," and another song called "Handful of Earth."

They practice the songs. Then there's a talk about mandatory overtime. And another about street credibility. They can pick up a supplementary check after the meeting and are taken to a back room where food is being collected for a food pantry. Rosa picks up some dried pinto beans and some rice. She knows a lot about surviving on beans and rice. At home in Xoyatla the meat usually ran out by the middle of the week, and then it was three or four days of beans and rice. It's laughable to think about these privations in her present circumstances, with their three salaries and the house paid off. While they're in the back room, Rosa asks Enedina about Wofie.

He was at the Sunshine Club today, Enedina tells her. No one know how he got there. They think Mrs. Hingy bring him maybe.

And the Fahey woman?

No one see her.

V.
Gina

The weekend is a little break from the strike. Dr. Garofalo comes in the gray Mercedes to pick her up and take her and Gina out to dinner in the North End.

Driving in from Storrow Drive through the narrow streets with shops below and apartments above, Gina notes how she could live here quite happily. They walk the streets for about half an hour, stopping in a silver shop where the doctor buys Gina a little box with curved legs like a dragon to hold her blood pressure pills, and Rosa a pretty hoop pendant on a pure silver chain. Rosa is overcome. She has never owned any expensive jewelry. Gina looks eagerly about as they walk in the fading light. Rosa guesses she is thinking it is like Italy here: here is the bakery and the tall church and the meat market. They go in a bakery and buy some pastries to take home. Rosa notes a pastry she knows from home, called *orejas*. Ears for elephants, she says, and the doctor buys her a half dozen. She tries to understand when the daughter talks to the mother in Italian, but there seem to be many words in Italian beyond the few she uses with Gina.

When they are seated inside the dim restaurant, the doctor translates what she was saying, something about a man who rode a horse along Lexington Road, where the buses ran, to Concord to warn the people the British were attacking, who was the same man who made the little pillbox she bought for Gina? No not that pillbox, but identical ones centuries ago...

Ah, says Rosa, who is cowed that moment by the tall waiter looming over them, severely waiting for their order. You choose for me, she tells the doctor, who takes her time ordering soup and a wine bottle that she must taste before she accepts it. There are some little artichokes with stuffing to eat in the meantime, along with a plate of olives and cheese. By the time Rosa has eaten a piece of cheese and two pieces of the crusty bread and finished the soup, a thick rich broth of what she tries not to think about being made from a turtle, she is uncomfortably full; but here the waiter is again, and she must decide if she wants fish or meat.

Well, a little fish maybe, but not too much, she tells the waiter, hoping he might smile, but he doesn't. He doesn't like I should be here, she decides.

The doctor is relaxing with the wine now and speaking animatedly in Italian with the waiter, lingering over the enormous menu.

You must try the polenta, she tells Rosa, and a large dish of this tamal-like substance arrives for them to share, along with a delicate fish on a bed of spinach for her and Gina and a large steak for the daughter. And this wasn't the end, for it was immediately followed by a liquor-flavored sherbet.

I will burst, Rosa thinks, for there was still dessert to come, and the stern waiter will be back; but the doctor orders her a soothing flan, which slips right down her throat, and which like the elephant ears was a regular part of her childhood. Then there is fruit and cheese, which Rosa can turn down in spite of the waiter's disapproval. She is a little drunk, and Gina's cheeks are flushed.

Driving home, the doctor invites her to sit up in the front seat so they can talk in English and discuss a possible time for Rosa to spend more hours with Gina. Rosa says she will think about it and closes her eyes as they pass through the narrow streets of three-story houses. She feels as if they are conspiring against Gina by speaking English.

Stop! Gina shrills suddenly from the back seat. Alarmed, her daughter pulls over and brakes.

What? What?

Un piso se alquila, Rosa understands. A flat for rent.

It seems Gina wants to get out of the car right here and rent a second-floor walk-up they just passed.

The daughter slows the car, leans her forehead on the steering wheel.

Mother of God, she moans.

Mother of God, shall I leave her here? she asks Rosa.

No, no, no! Gina is trying to open the locked door.

The doctor controls herself and pulls out again calmly. No, Mother, you cannot live here, she tells Gina.

While Gina sobs and chokes in the back, they stop at a light, and the daughter says to Rosa, You see how bad it is...?

Yes, yes, Rosa says, feeling badly for Gina. But what can anyone do?

I haven't told her this yet, but I have the house up for sale, the doctor says, shocking Rosa.

I'll have to take a loss on a house I've only owned a year, but if it isn't too big a loss, I'm doing it. We shall live over a store downtown. It's the only solution, unless I fill my yard with goats and chickens...

Rosa, whose womb had been aching for Gina, now aches for the daughter. Her beautiful house! She thinks of telling her how she, Rosa, once lived very happily over a store in Billerica, but decides not to.

If Rosa's own mother had lived, she thinks, and needed to come to her, she would want just what Gina wants: either the animals nearby, or the bakery and the church and the bodega where you could send a child with a handful of change to buy a lemon.

Yes, she feels a sadness for those big houses in Lexington. They are too far apart. The daughter must understand.

As she gets ready for bed after this eventful day, she casts around in her mind for a place downtown where Gina might be happy and suddenly thinks of the Hampton Gardens where Wolfie lives. She recalls the pretty brickwork and the graceful old doors. On the first floor there is a large oil painting of a town falling down a hill to a line of boat docks that must be in Italy somewhere. Is Gina too rich to go to the Sunshine Club? There, Rosa could talk to her in Spanish, and Mrs. Rose can speak Spanish, she knows! And mother and daughter will both realize what a fine lady Mrs. Rose is, who entertained a president of Venezuela once. And Wolfie, she will tell them how Wolfie lives in the Hampton Gardens, and was a famous lawyer and helped many people... And he has wealthy sons who can buy him a talking machine that must be very expensive... Her mind is so busy with these thoughts she can't fall asleep until close to dawn, tired as she is.

Next day is Sunday, luckily, so she can stay in bed late and go to a later Mass. And Father Aidan preaches a very nice sermon about how old Abraham banishes his servant Hagar and her son Ishmael she had with Abraham back when Sarah was barren. They were sent into the wilderness where they will surely die; but God has compassion on Hagar. She can look right at him, which nobody can do and not die, and He tells her that both of them will be taken care of and Ishmael shall prosper and head a whole tribe of people. He goes on to talk about how sometimes bad happenings can lead to better things you never expected. Exactly what she was thinking last night, Rosa realizes.

She won't go to the Spanish Mass anymore, she thinks. Father Aidan she can understand better than Father Riley anyhow; and she won't have to listen to the Mexicans' toneless singing their little songs and displaying their Virgins all over the place, and the gringos' *disparates*.

And, as always lately, she is thinking about how she can practice talking to Wolfie when she sees him, and learn more words and better ways to put them together. And she can sleep later, too, she thinks gratefully, for this strike is wearing everybody out.

Next day, before showing up for her shift, Rosa has to go to the Municipal Building to pick up the papers for getting legal. Coming down the steps in the sun, she decides she has time to walk back to Hampton Gardens and see the downtown as Gina will see it when she moves here: the Banks Square Market that sells Italian ices in the summer, the elementary school, so there will be children; and, passing Hampton Gardens again, she notes the circular garden around a Virgin that is full of those spikey red flowers that are all over in the Italian neighborhoods out by Piety Corner, and thinks again of the oil painting of the little town spilling down the hill above a bunch of red boats that hangs in the lobby and must look like Italy. Then there is the Waltham Supermarket, and the library with English classes in the basement and all the stored dusty books in French with their leather bindings—maybe some Italian ones among them for all the Italians that came along with the French from Canada to work in the mill. And Mama Josie's, which has a Greek owner but serves Italian food, and the Shawmut Bank with all the things going on in the city running around its sign:

Harpsichord Concert...

at City Hall...

Saturday Evening...

May 15, 7 PM...

...Scarlatti...

And the big white Congregational church with the soup kitchen in the basement, and the Haitian church in the chapel, and the loud Latino Pentecostals... and the French church and its bingo hall—the Italian church is too far, unfortunately. Rosa used to think enviously of how the city accommodated the French and the Irish and the Italians but not her own people; still, she sees there are efforts, like the English classes and the rented chapels, and the Mexican stores creeping in. There's one on Moody Street now.

Could Gina walk as far as Moody Street from Hampton Gardens? Then she could pass O'Reilly's Daughter and see the girl who comes out of her little house and waves a red flag at the train crossing, and the Commons, where she could rest on a bench and see the buses and the trains letting people off and on, and feed the pigeons, and look at the statues, and maybe see some picketers. Or rest in the little park where the old movie theater was and look down at the river, or look in the windows of Grover Cronin's, or even go in and buy some perfume or a hanky, and go in to see the Industry Museum at the Old Mill, with its electric cars that were built here, and the pieces of the old looms and the clocks and watches, and finally have a cup of coffee and a pastry in the ... Rosa is overwhelmed suddenly with the riches of her city and the thrills that await Gina. She finds herself all the way up to the Irish Travel Bureau before she walks back to the bus stop and looks at it all again:

Dot Slamin Hill ...

American Legion Band ...

Concert on Waltham Common ...

May 18

VI.
Go Down Moses

Rosa sees with her own eyes that it's Mrs. Hingy brings Wolfie on Monday when it's her day to bring Clifford and Alcide—Alcide has disappeared again.

And things at the Sunshine Club are far gone, Rosa notes with alarm. A look in the kitchen sets her to cleaning up as much as she can, but there are too many people needing to go to the bathroom. Two Social Services people are helping, and they try to tell her she shouldn't be here.

I must be here, Rosa tells them, walking away.

Rebecca has given up on Reality Orientation, and some consumers are listlessly coloring or cutting out pictures with the dull scissors, and the rest are watching the *Today Show* on TV. Every so often the news comes on and shows pictures of the strikers.

Wolfie and Clifford are being sent to a nursing home sometime this morning, Rebecca tells her.

Wolfie is sitting next to Bobby Rosier, so Rosa moves him over by Mrs. Rose.

They've given him a catheter, she notices. Why does he need a catheter? And it looks like he's wearing a diaper...

So have they made you an offer? Mrs. Rose asks.

Rosa doesn't understand.

More money. The agencies.

Ah, of course that's what it's all about. A couple of dollars more a day. How can this cause so much bad things to happen ...?

She tells Mrs. Rose she doesn't know.

Then the men from the Chair Car Service come in for Clifford and Wolfie. She thought she'd be relieved when this happened—he'd be out of the Fahey woman's reach—but instead she's frightened: the catheter, the diaper, the distant look on his face ... Usually he listened eagerly to Mrs. Rose's talk, but not today. Oh, this must end. She will sneak to the agency and tell them to take her back. The union can have her check back and the beans and rice and the sign ... She sits by Mrs. Rose, overcome.

I've seen many strikes in my day—from the other side of course—but my sympathies were always with the workers, Rosa hears Mrs. Rose say. You must be brave, my dear. Rosa wonders for a moment, does Mrs. Rose know about her, about Wolfie?

It's especially hard, I imagine, for you people; for you're not interfering with the assembly belt production of some product, some can or bottle of something ... but with helpless ...

Yes, Rosa says, looking into Mrs. Rose's light blue eyes, so unlike her own people's, and seeing her kindness; she is undone.

I love Wolfie, she blurts. Now she's done it! He help us get legal and all, she adds.

I know, I know, but he'll be taken care of. And just think he would want you to do this—I suspect he's pinko like me, and I'm kind of enjoying not having to undergo Reality Orientation for a while, and watching this all on the news. We'll be all right; and if you don't need that raise, some of the others do, so be brave another day, can you?

Rosa is crying, and Henrietta Rose has put her arms around her. Any other day this would have been taken notice of, but not today.

Another strike day, she thinks, waiting for the Boston and Maine to pull through the crossing so she can join the others assembling by the bus stop.

Priscilla is talking through a bullhorn. There's been an offer of a dollar fifty cents more on beginning hourly wages, and benefits for part-timers who work twenty hours. We plan to reject it.

Reject it! someone shouts. Then more people:

Not good enough!

Strike! Strike!

Rosa wonders if some of them think the checks and the cans of beans and the free hot dogs will go on forever and they can live on that.

She should have asked the chair car men where they were taking Wolfie. There are six or so nursing homes in the city. She'll have to check them all.

Three more days of marching. All of the agencies are out now. People gather in the Common and look at them with a bit of respect. The Kisser and some other harmless people released from the State have been told they can't join the strikers. No more kids either, only workers' children and the kids from Brandeis who are equipped with their own signs—not as nice as their own, Rosa notes.

But many of the signs are in tatters, and Mondo is working on new ones on the kitchen table at night.

Wolfie will be proud, say Mrs. Rose. But he'll also forget how to go to the bathroom mostly by himself. His arms will go weak. And no one in a nursing home is going to understand that talking machine ... It will probably be stolen, along with his soft shirts and his flannel pants, and his expensive ties, and his motorized wheelchair.

Maybe the son ... surely the son.

She calls three nursing homes and is told by each one that such information can only be released to family. The Hazelwood Manor is on her way home, so she gets off the bus and goes in and asks to see Mr. Wolf.

There's no Wolf here, she's told. She has to wait an hour for the next bus.

Friday, she can go to help Rebecca.

She catches Alcide before he escapes and gives him a bath. He's filthy.

Where have you been? she asks.

I have a job, he says.

What job?

I put on a chicken suit and wave my wings in front of the Golden Hen. He waves his forearms and wags his behind to demonstrate.

No! She can't imagine anything more revolting.

They pay you?

Two dollar an hour and all I can eat. Chicken, chicken, chicken.

Well, you going to the Sunshine Club today, or I report you.

Hokay.

There are only six people left at the Sunshine Club. Some high school volunteers try to make them sing. No one wants to. Mrs. Rose can play the harp, Rosa suggests.

The harp is found in a storage room. Oh, stop yer racket, Terry complains. The others fall asleep. Rebecca is assigned to the kitchen now. She has no time to stir people up. Rosa takes people to the bathroom, then goes to help Rebecca.

All the food is dumped right from the government cans into the kettles.

Peas the color of army fatigues, little hard potatoes, smelling of the can, little hard meatballs in tomato sauce, also smelling of can. How can they give this food to Mrs. Rose, who has eaten at the tables of presidents? No wonder Alcide run away. She would run away too. She was quite fond of the food from the Golden Hen, and sometimes brought home a box of chicken parts for a treat.

For weeks, it seems, she's been standing on her feet, never having time to say more than six words to anybody. What are all these words about: mandatory overtime? Who is this godlike Andy Stern? Suppose little Esmeralda wants to interview her about all this; what can she say?

On Sunday, after Mass, Mondo drives her to Priscilla's with some new signs. New signs mean more strike, thinks Rosa. But the checks have stopped coming, so that's a good sign.

Not a good sign for Priscilla, though. Again Rosa is all mixed up in her loyalties.

Guilty all around.

Then, the next week right before the meeting, she finds Priscilla uncharacteristically flat on her back on one of the rackety beds she calls futons in the back room she calls her office.

Rosa is ready for the union talk: negotiations, collective bargaining, mandatory overtime, Andy Stern, the SEIU, street credibility . . . but Priscilla, who likes to talk Spanish with Rosa, greets her with these words: *Mi hija esta preñada.*

Soledad. Rosa takes this calmly.

Sí, sí, de Nelson Márquez.

Nelson Márquez is the juvenile delinquent that Priscilla used to try to teach how to read at the Service Center in the project. Priscilla gets up then and goes into the kitchen to make them some tea.

I make, Rosa says, and makes Priscilla sit at the table. She looks like she's been crying, Rosa can see.

Mondo stands around embarrassed. She hasn't even looked at his signs. *Cretino*, he says of Nelson Márquez.

It's not that he's Latino, Priscilla says to Mondo.

You like it better if it's me, Mondo says.

She looks at him and laughs. They are like friends, Rosa notes with pleasure.

Maybe I would, Priscilla says, cheering up a little. I'm not even sure it's Nelson. She put out his name when she first told me, later she says it might be his brother. I think she said Nelson to hurt me, because I used to pay him so much attention. I loved Nelson. I love him. But he's fucking fifteen. Solie is sixteen.

My Lidia sixteen too, when she get that way. She all right now, though, says Rosa, not sure this will help.

She wants to keep it, Priscilla goes on, as if still going over all this in her mind. That made me feel a little better, oddly. It's that, it's that...

Rosa stands to get the boiling kettle. The kitchen is so small she doesn't need to take a step.

...that divorcing her stepdad and having to move into the project was all my idea. No one ever asked for her opinion, even though she was only six years old at the time. Solie has hated everything I've done for the past ten years. She tries all the time to punish me. You want to live with Puerto Ricans... forgive me, Rosa. You choose to live here, then this is what you get... Well, she could have put up with it, she could have reasoned she'd wait it out till she gets a scholarship like Frostie—she could do it easy—and get out, go to her stepdad's, go on her own...

Like your Eva, Rosa. You don't have to be as bad as the worst of them here, but that's what she does, to get back at me...

That's okay, that's okay. Priscilla puts her head into her hands. She can hate me all she wants. But who is she punishing now? Not me. Herself. That's why I'm so sad.

It work out, Rosa says. You will see.

Maybe it will, Priscilla says softly. Maybe, if she keeps it. She was playing around with these families. To get back at me. But now she's hitched herself up for real. More hitched than I'll ever be just by living here in the projects. She's more like me now, maybe. Maybe we can understand each other. She's like me, I tell her. We do everything the hard way...

Mondo has been listening to this. Maybe thinking a little bit about mothers and their sorrows, Rosa hopes.

She ain't gonna marry Nelson Márquez, he says.

Nelson Márquez is fifteen, Priscilla says. He still can't read. He steals. But maybe it's Ángel, the big brother. He's okay. It's a good family. Ramona and I between us can handle another baby. She's got fourteen. What's one more? I got three; what's another one ... Solie can stay in school. She can go to college ...

Good, yes, good, Rosa says. A baby is a good thing. Go to college good thing. All good ...

But Rosa, I have to give her some attention right now, and there's this strike, Priscilla says.

I hate this strike, pops out of Rosa's mouth.

Priscilla isn't listening. There's been another offer ... about two dollars more an hour. They didn't budge on benefits ... It's not bad for a start, but I can't let my personal problems make the decision; I mean, the leadership will go along with me if I decide ... but how can I let my personal ...

Let them, thinks Rosa. But she says nothing. Day after tomorrow is the eighth of May, long past her day to go to Wolfie. She's ashamed of herself for thinking this.

Her bleeding starts next morning. Some pain, not bad. Wolfie will find me as he left me, she thinks. Her womb flutters.

It's over, Lidia calls from the kitchen where she has the little TV.

The strike? Rosa cries from the bedroom.

Yeah, answers Mondo, who's in the kitchen too. You got your two bucks an hour.

PART FOUR

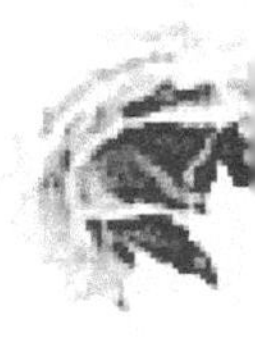

I.
Going to Wolfie

Rosa gets dressed hurriedly: I must find him today, she tells herself. In the little time she had left to herself during the strike she had walked into the two closest nursing homes, the one on Myrtle and the one on Route 20, asking to see Mr. Wolf without success. It leaves the three out near Piety Corner.

Rosa walks.

She doesn't even check in at the agency first. She must go now.

She walks. It's a warm day. The summer birds are back with their songs. She notes all the little buds ready to burst: yellow forsythia, pink laurel. Trees are shedding bright green winged seeds that lay over the verge where she walks, filling the gutter. She notes the little crocus spears with their purple swelling pressing against the green casing, a tiny white flower already out, a single glove, a rusted battery, a bicycle tire, a gray stone with a white stripe through it, the dry plumes of last year's goldenrod. She is pleasantly conscious all the way of her tender breasts, her heavy cramping womb, going to Wolfie.

She must tell him right away that he must do things for himself, so this will never happen again. Maybe the next strike she can put her whole heart into then. No, probably not: there will still be Mrs. Rose and Alcide and …

There is the Kisser coming toward her. She never saw him quite this far from town before. He's wearing his Red Sox uniform, recently washed it looks. He is smiling, and his plump cheeks are rosy, his black hair slicked back. Maybe he's been in the hospital. Getting cleaned up and fed regular.

The kiss comes. Soft and friendly. Her womb doesn't rise. Rosa smiles at him. Good morning, she says. He makes a little bow.

I will carry this kiss to Wolfie, she thinks, walking on.

Wolfie's catheter must come out. Rosa feels powerful enough to make this happen. She will accompany him to the bathroom for a time, but she will make him learn to open his pants by himself, and stand, like a man, holding the rail. If he can open her blouse, then he can open his pants. Then the cooking … she will try to teach him to make simple things, like the fried egg sandwiches Leo makes for Winnie …

She crosses Nonantum Street and waits for the light to cross Lexington Road. She will try Braeburn Manor first. It is the nicest one, at least from the outside. She feels certain it is the right one, that his son has seen to it he went there.

Braeburn Manor is surrounded by old laurel bushes. Every year when Rosa sees laurels about to burst out, she always thinks of them as crying out: *Gloria al Padre!*

Thus she crosses herself as she passes by them going up the steps to the wide porch. He will be here, she knows.

Mr. Wolf? Yes, he is here, says a busy girl at the front desk. The wallpaper in the foyer is all pink roses. They are raised and have a texture like peach fuzz. Nice, thinks Rosa, a nice place.

I am his fren, begins Rosa. No! she exclaims. He my consumer. The agency give ... him ... me ... today. Her English is getting all *loco*.

Well, we've heard nothing about that ...

Rosa is becoming unsure.

But if you're his friend you can go in and visit if you wait till ten, the girl says.

It's only eight o'clock by the wall clock in front of her.

But I can wash him. I can do him. Save you the ...

Sorry. I can't let you.

Rosa has nothing to distract her during the next two hours. At first they seem longer than the entire strike seemed, when she could wait patiently. Breakfast trays pass her, awaking hunger. She hasn't even eaten before coming. Fool, she thinks. And how she must look, sitting there idly, to her own people, the aides, who rush about with trays and bedpans. Well, maybe they think she's waiting to be hired. She sits up straighter, like a prospective employee, her pocketbook held primly in her lap. She doesn't move from this position for two hours. Her eyes unfocused, waiting. The old tribal patience comes back to her. The old habit of sitting on your haunches leaning against the front wall of a house of whitewashed *bejareque*, wrapped in a blanket, looking at a dirt trail, waiting for a bus.

So she isn't even thinking of Wolfie when the girl at the desk—a nice girl really, Rosa doesn't fault her for following the rules—says to her, it's five after ten.

She goes timidly down a hall and up a staircase. Room 215.

There's a commotion in the room. He's pulled out the catheter. Oh, good for him, thinks Rosa. But how it must hurt! He's lying exposed there on the bed, nearly naked, while they swab his penis with brown Betadine. And they haven't even pulled the curtains round the bed. You can see by his face what it must have cost him to do this thing to himself.

Oh, leave it out, Rosa pleads to a young aide. The girl looks at her blankly. It's none of her decision.

Leave him, she says with more authority. I take care of him. I licensed nurse aide. So they leave him. What do they care ... It's probably their break time.

His eyes are closed. His brow gathering up the fierce pain. Rosa closes the curtain around him. There is a moribund-looking man in the next bed. Then she covers him with a sheet and draws up the wooden chair and sits by him, holding his hand. It hurt, she says. I know it hurt.

She is patient. After all her impatience she has found patience. Little by little, the brow smooths out, the eyes open. The dear man.

Neither speaks. Probably a half hour passes. The face becomes Wolfie's. Nee go, he says finally.

She doesn't see his motorized chair; but there is a regular wheelchair next to the other man's bed. She helps him sit up and swings his legs to the floor, carefully covering his lower body with a sheet. When he's able to stay upright she goes to the closet and finds a black running suit. Brandeis University, it reads, front and back and down the legs. This she puts on him, covering his naked parts all the while with the sheet. She might have been dressing a royal person, except there's a foolish smile on her face the whole time.

Goo…, he says, and almost smiles.

You go back home, she says. And never come here again, she says.

He can barely stand. Probably he's been in bed the entire strike. But Rosa's embrace is steady, and she lifts and swings him into the wheelchair.

She takes him into the bathroom, leaving the door open, helps him onto the toilet. The standing part can wait.

He can't urinate, though he strains. But he's had his way. Coming in here to go in the toilet was part of his plan. He must have worked at the catheter over days, secretly, pulling and enduring as much pain as he could, then waiting to try again, slowly working it out. Or maybe, she doesn't know, he yanked it out all at once.

She gently washes his face, smoothing away the strain. Then his back. The skin is still white and unblemished, like creamy stationery, his hair still black black, falling over his forehead.

No one comes. He should have something for the pain, for the possible infection. His breakfast tray is gone cold sitting in the corner. They've simply abandoned him to her.

Never come back here, she says over and over, almost singing it.

She gives him some mouthwash to swish around in his mouth. She combs his hair, grown quite long over his ears. A hand cups her breast as she reaches over to make his right-sided part. She closes her eyes a moment and feels her womb squeeze … still the old Wolfie … still the old Wolfie, jaunty in his Brandeis running outfit.

But she won't let him inside her clothes today. She is all business now. She wheels him to the nurses' station. There's no one there, but the med cart is down the hall, and she finds the head nurse in the end room. He need pain pill, she says, standing in the door with Wolfie in the chair.

What?

He need pain med. He pull out his catheter.

What!

Is true.

Oh, my God!

Nobody tol' you?

No, no.

Only after the nurse has gone back to the meds room and called the doctor and found Wolfie something for pain does the woman ask who is Rosa. It seems once you wait till ten o'clock you can do anything you want in here.

They wait for the pain med, alone in the room with the probably dead man in the other bed. No one comes, not even to help the dead man reach his tray.

Will Wolfie eat something? Rosa brings the other cold tray over.

No, no, he tells her, giving her his hand to hold and closing his eyes.

Thinking he probably can't be listening to her through his pain, Rosa begins to talk.

First, she tells him about Esmeralda. A very smart little girl. She 'splain to me all about my people, how they have fine temples and pyramids and a language they figure out, that is not Spanish, and about where it come ... came from, and where is Spain, and Italy and the Mediterranean Sea.

And I try to tell her about my life, which I never think about before. And I have to find the parts that a little girl can hear. This is not easy; but there are parts I can tell ... about how I come here.

And all the time these things happen to me. Like I come to know a woman who only speak Italian and I can understand her, almost, and so her daughter, an important doctor, is become my friend, and A Big Thing, I find out I am legal, for live with a Puerto Rican man enough years. And he die ... died, died, died ... so I am a widow and people can respect me. And his children love me, and I can help them even when I can't help my own in no way. Any, any, any ...

Anyway ... But I am all *loca*, Rosa tells herself, hoping Wolfie hasn't been listening. But she looks at him and he seems to be almost smiling, so she blunders on.

Anyway, I study the English, because now I am a widow, and a legal person, and I know people like Mrs. Rose who is good to me, and the Doctor Daughter who is respecting me ...

He is smiling, the poor man.

So I am ashamed. I was a good student when I was a girl. I am the fastest reader of my sisters. My first English teacher in the basement of the library let me speak as bad as I wanted, like the Polish people who suffered in the war and never had any lessons until they got very old.

But now I have a new teacher, she is Miss Ann Marie, and she makes us say the wrong things the right way. And as many times the right way as we said the wrong . . . or almost.

And I have to say anymore, anymore, anymore . . . over and over Out Loud, and people in the street think I am saying hello.

Wolfie is smiling, she thinks, so she says it again:

Anymore anymore . . .

Yes, he is smiling, even though his brow is still knit together in pain.

And there is a man on the streets for years. I not . . . I don't know if you ever see him. But if women are not careful and paying attention he kiss you on the mouth, and two times now he catch me.

Wolfie's belly contracts in the beginning of a chuckle that doesn't quite make a sound.

And finally, the nurse comes and gives Wolfie a shot in his hip. Rosa waits awhile and then wheels him out into the hall.

Now he must eat. He will eat today, she thinks, noting again how thin he's gotten. You can see his bones even through the thick running suit. How often did his tray just sit on the other side of the room getting cold?

She stands in the hall with his wheelchair firmly gripped. Then she tells an aide, he must eat. His breakfast cold.

I get new one, the girl says. An alert girl. Resembles Esmeralda. One of her people. The girl goes herself to the kitchen and brings a tray into the day room, where there are a few patients lolling over their trays. One woman looks at them with a bright, demented stare. Rosa wheels Wolfie up to her table.

This is Mr. Wolf, she says to the woman in the victorious voice that has come into her since ten o'clock. You will like to talk to him. He is a known-well lawyer in this town, who help many people ... many people.